I0677872

NINE FINE DEATHS

Even when you know who
the killer is, you won't know
who the killer is

A novel

S.E. Mills

PUBLISHERS OF O.G AUTHOR GENIUSES

Published by E&R Publishers
New York, NY, USA

An imprint of MillsiCo Publishing, USA
www.EandR.pub

Copyright: © 2025 S.E. Mills. All rights reserved.

Your guarantee of quality

As publishers, we strive to produce every book to the highest commercial standards. The printing and binding have been planned to ensure a sturdy, attractive publication that should provide years of enjoyment. If your copy fails to meet our high standards, please inform us, and we will gladly replace it.

admin@millsi.co

ISBN: 9781966155010 (Hardcover)
ISBN: 9781966155041 (Paperback)
ISBN: 9781966155058 (Ebook)
ISBN: 9781966155065 (Audiobook)

Library of Congress Control Number: 2025932834

First Edition

Contents

Murder One

The courtyard of the historic Apthorp building on the Upper West Side was an inch deep in water when the police arrived. A Coca-Cola bottling truck had backed into a hydrant because of the double-parked asshole blocking him in due to his urgent need for another burnt cup of coffee-flavored dishwater from Starbucks on Broadway and 78th. The circular driveway was jammed with police cars, an ambulance, and a laundry truck that couldn't get out—the driver was pissed and cursing at everyone. Detective Bradley wandered over to settle him down.

"Good morning!"

"Who the fuck are you with your good fucking morning, lady? fuck you, I've got places to be," demanded the irate and impatient truck driver.

"Oh, you do? The police lockup is a place to be. That's where I take people for disturbing the peace or just being an impatient asshole at a murder scene who pisses me off," Detective Bradley was in no mood for this asshole.

"Murder?"

"You'll be out of here soon. Calm your tits."

"Yes, ma'am."

"Call me that again, and I will just shoot you and save myself a trip to the station."

"Yes, officer."

"Detective."

"Noted! Crazy bitch," he whispered into his gloves.

Detective Bradley stopped and turned back to stare him down.

"Not so much of the bitch, bitch, and if you want to see crazy, you've come to the right fucking town and met the right fucking person."

He slunk begrudgingly up into his truck and sat quietly.

Madeline Bradley was one bitter Detective. She had some success as a banker in North London, came to New York, failed as a real estate developer, became a broker, failed, and finally became interested in police work while being investigated for mortgage fraud. After outsmarting the investigators, they suggested she would make a great detective. She took it seriously, and with her high-level development and political connections, she got a fast track through the system, and two years later, she was Detective Third Grade Bradley. Bradley loved the freedom, wandering the city and working out which motherfucker killed which motherfucker. She could easily get inside the mind of a killer because she had always toyed with the romantic notion of becoming a hitter. Killing people for a living was her dream job for releasing her wellspring of rage.

*   *   *

Apartment 41D was magnificent. The millwork was not painted but encased in a waxed shellac. The dining table was a grand centerpiece, hand-carved in Thailand. It had a glass top with a wonderous lost city carved under the glass in relief. Atop the spectacular table was the victim, perfectly posed as if being served for a state dinner. Her head was bound tightly in lunch wrap, and her perfectly formed naked body featured an array of small, multicolored porcelain dishes containing various dipping sauces.

The first thought that came into Bradley's mind was how hungry she was, having skipped breakfast and feeling decidedly dusty from a heavy evening of Long Island ice teas.

She had not seen that many dead bodies in her short tenure as a detective, but it just didn't seem to affect her. Death and the dead were as traumatic as driftwood to her.

"Judging by the price of apartments in this building, she was either into finance, fraud, or philanderers."

"She was a diamond dealer," boomed a new voice in the room. The voice belonged to an old Jewish gentleman who had just walked in.

"So, all three then," quipped Bradley to herself.

She caught herself quickly, realizing that this man must be a friend of the victim, also in the diamond business. He was glaring at Bradley with disdain but chose not to engage.

"So, what can you tell me about her?"

"Alexis was my protégé. Alexis Anne Riccardi. She knew computers and had opened international opportunities for our diamond exchange. She was diligent, had no enemies, and made us all very wealthy. I can't believe somebody would do this to her. She was a bright, beautiful, and innocent young lady."

Are any of us really innocent? Bradley thought to herself.

"No forced entry, no struggle, no signs of theft. She must have let the killer in, and she must have known him, or there would have been some sort of resistance."

Bradley walked over to the kitchen trash can and stomped the pedal, popping up the lid. She bent over and fished out a pink N95 mask, which was still slightly damp.

"So, he gave her the mask, which was dowsed with trichloromethane; she would have gone down in seconds. He wrapped her head in Cling Wrap—classy—and posed her on the table while she unconsciously suffocated. I mean, you have to admire the cleanliness of it all."

The other officers stared at Bradley in stunned, silent disbelief.

"What? Well, you do have to admit it's a pretty tidy death scene. I have cleaning ladies who leave the place in worse shape than this! I'd hire this guy in a heartbeat."

The medics rolled in the gurney and started to prep the body.

"Are we all done here, detective?" The EMT stood with hands poised over the dipping dishes on the victim's naked body.

"Yes, we've gotten all the clues we're getting from this girl."

Bradley went down to the lobby to check who had signed in that morning. One plumber, one personal trainer, and one gentleman visitor. All three were still in the building, so Bradley had them come into the building conference room for an interview.

Each had impervious alibis except for the plumber. The resident had gone out and left him to his work, but he was 63 years old, covered in plumber grime, and very confused about why Bradley was talking to him.

Bradley knew that this guy would have left a trail that a blind man could follow, and he just didn't fit this in any way. This was either another resident or somebody who got into the building undetected.

Cameras only covered the lobby, and there were three other entrances to the building. The gymnasium, the trades entrance, and the parking garage. They would have needed a key to get in through any of these entrances, and trades all had to sign in before being let into the trades entrance, so this left only other residents.

"What makes you think this is a man?"

A heavy-set black man stood at the door of the conference room.

"Well, hello, Captain America."

"I told you not to call me that, Bradley. Merrick, Captain Merrick, Carl, if we were friends, but Captain Merrick will do you just fine."

"Noted. Well, I just don't see a woman using Cling Wrap as a murder weapon. We're more knife and poison types, you know. I mean, it's elegant but not lady elegant. This was a man. A man who thinks he has a sense of humor. Dipping dishes. Chicks just don't think like that. You need a man for that kind of bizarre weirdry."

"Okay, well, get it written up, and let's see what we can do about profiling the 1287 residents of this completely fucked up building full of rich people."

A total of 112 people were without alibis, were male, and were able to walk with some sort of flexibility, but after 112 interviews, none of them were a fit for this murder. Without the killer just showing up and admitting it, this case was dead in the water. *Of course,* thought Bradley to herself, *we can just wait for the next one. Somebody this outlandish doesn't stop at one.*

Reynaldo—The Tree Guy

1979. Hollywood Hills, California

TJ stood at his island bench washing dishes after a long day of writing. He was working from home because the studio staff found him brash, abrasive, opinionated, and obnoxious. They knew he was brilliant and great at his job—good writers were really hard to find—but the studio heads were sick of the complaints, so they encouraged TJ to work from home.

It's not that he didn't like people; he did; he didn't like people who were phoning it in, lacking in talent, or intellectually unworthy.

"TJ," said Simone, the person responsible for bringing him into the gig. "Kelvin said you are becoming impossible to work with."

"No, dude, it's impossible to work with Kelvin because he doesn't do any fucking work. It's not that I don't respect him; disrespect would take up energy; he's just a nothing. Ignoring him and his ideas is not a challenge; he is basically invisible to me. I'm just getting it done, man."

"But we are a team; how do you expect the team to be productive if you won't talk to them?"

"Talking or not talking, the outcome will be the same; if you want a better team, hire more people like me. I'd rather pick up trash or clean toilets than listen to his stupid-ass ideas. Ya, feel me?"

"I do feel ya, TJ. I feel ya working from home!"

And so, here he was, working from home. Like it was some punishment. *My disdain for lesser minds may be offensive to the lesser minds, but I just don't give a fuck,* he thought to himself. He didn't care if people called him a narcissist as long as they didn't call him.

As he stood at his kitchen sink washing his breakfast, lunch, and dinner dishes, he was completely unaware he was being watched. In The Hills, you either have a sharp relief with a view down or an extreme incline in your backyard. Sometimes both. TJ's backyard was intensely steep, with terraced platforms and stairs between them.

Many nights, TJ would look out his window to see coyotes trotting by on trails through his backyard. He loved living with wildlife all around him. Animals, from hummingbirds to deer, would frequent his home. TJ was houseproud and loved taking care of it, upgrading it, renovating it, painting it, and caring for the trees. The trees were especially difficult because they were rooted in the steep banks and curved sharply upward, seeking the sun. One palm tree in particular towered 150 feet into the air, and the leaves at the top needed semi-regular trimming. This was way out of TJ's comfort zone, so he had to hire someone.

Reynaldo knocked on TJs door early one Monday morning. He was a tall, slight, but wiry-looking fellow.

"Sir, I am Reynaldo. The tree guy. I am here for the trees."

"Oh yeah, yeah, the tree guy, nice, come in, man. I keep the trees outside."

Reynaldo didn't pay any attention to TJ's humor. He had his own agenda. TJ stood back in amazement as Reynaldo scaled the 150-foot palm and trashed the dead leaves from the top with a machete. He was freaked out just looking at him all the way up there with the tree bending and swaying wildly.

Reynaldo didn't care about the height or the risk. He didn't feel fear; in fact, he found it exhilarating to do things that other people wouldn't dream of doing, and he found it easy. This job gave him some very specific advantages that he loved, and one of those advantages was watching. He would sometimes stay up in his perch for hours, just watching people in the windows all around him.

One evening, Reynaldo was working on TJ's trees, and he noticed the coyotes trotting through. He watched where they went and saw that they had trails all through these hills. This gave Reynaldo an idea that would put him on a path he never expected but would serve his unquenchable thirst to observe people.

Over the following months, Reynaldo mapped his intricate network of clients' homes, the trees from where he could observe, and the paths that connected his labyrinth through the Hollywood Hills. He could observe the residents of all the homes like it was an ant farm.

Very late one night, much later than he usually finished at TJ's house, while perched up on the high palm he saw something strange. He had been up there for hours dreaming and observing. At first, he was just watching a beautiful woman undress while watching herself in the mirror. Her sensual moves were exciting for him, and he wanted to take a closer look. After shimmying down the 100-foot tower, he took one of the trails that the coyotes take, which led him across the road and up the adjacent bank. He made his way up the steep incline and up a large eucalyptus tree, which gave him a perfect view into her bedroom.

When he got comfortable, he turned toward the window expecting to see his beautiful naked target, but instead, he saw a man staring right at him. Or so he thought. He froze, thinking he had been discovered, but as he clung to his tether, frozen in place, hardly breathing, he realized that the man was not staring at him but out into space as if daydreaming. He hung there with his locked gaze for at least five minutes before the man seemed to come to as if waking suddenly from a dream. The tall figure turned and walked away. There, lying on the floor behind where the man stood, was the naked body of the woman. Motionless, with her head twisted in an unnatural pose. Reynaldo knew it didn't look right. He felt something he was not used to feeling: fear.

He watched for several minutes to see if the man had left the house, but he didn't see him, so he quietly lowered himself down the tree, back down the trail, and back to the road. He walked up the hill to where he had parked his truck, got in, started it, and drove slowly down it. As he drove past the house he had been watching, he saw that same man coming out the front door and walking down the front steps. He looked away, trying not to lock eyes. Just a gardener driving home in his truck at the end of the day. Reynaldo got to the corner, turned right, and increased speed to put some distance between himself and the murderer; his voyeuristic penchant quelled indefinitely.

Murder Two

Bradley awoke to the terrifying sound of a smoke alarm shrieking at 120 decibels. She had left a loaf of bread inside the plastic on top of the drip-filter coffee machine, which had automatically turned on at 6 AM, heated up the bread, melted the plastic, created toxic smoke, and triggered the alarm.

She frantically threw her exhausted, hungover body into action, grabbed her gun—always expecting the worst—and ran into the kitchen. Once she established that nobody was there and that she had caused the problem herself, she turned and shot the smoke alarm off the ceiling. It smashed into the wall and landed in pieces on the floor, still screaming. Bradley stood over it, looking down like it was a slimeball she'd just apprehended, but instead of an arrest, she pointed the gun at the screaming bitch of a thing and pulled the trigger. Finally silenced, she kicked the remaining pieces out of the way to reveal the bullet embedded in her hardwood floor.

"Shut the fuck up, you screaming fucking bitch!"

The day had begun. Her cell phone rang.

"Good morning, Captain Am..., Captain Am, Captain, Am I going to be happy with the news you're calling me about."

"Probably," said Merrick. "You seem to love dead bodies. 410 Park. 10th floor. Looks like your guy again."

"Why's that?"

"You'll see."

Bradley took the elevator inside her apartment to the parking garage. One of the reasons she rented this place was that its strange configuration allowed for a private elevator to the parking garage. Any architect would say it was a design flaw, but this happy accident of her apartment being orphaned by the rest of the building due to some strange city egress law was just perfect for her.

Her silver Range Rover police car sat in its usual spot by the elevator door. She climbed in and made her way from the West Side Highway to Park Avenue.

Bradley just loved the freedom that police work afforded her. Nowhere to park? No problem. Just get out in the middle of Park Avenue and block a whole lane.

Her head was pounding even worse than usual, possibly from the early morning close-range gunfire. The rattly elevator was making her queasy as her alcohol-battered equilibrium struggled to keep her upright.

Apartment 10C was taped off, and the medics were standing outside waiting for Bradley. They would never enter a crime scene ahead of her again; after that time, she grabbed Luis firmly by his junk for corrupting the scene at an Upper East Side apartment robbery a few months back. He had bruised testicles for days after. Luis stood back with his hands together, covering his crotch as Bradley looked at him with her knowing smirk.

"What doooo we have here, boys?" Bradley quipped melodically.

Bradley walked in with inappropriate enthusiasm, followed by the mystified medics.

"Stay back, man. That bitch is unbalanced."

"I'm balanced," retorted Bradley, giving no argument to the "bitch" reference.

The medics looked at each other with surprise that she could hear their whispers from 20 feet back.

"Well?"

Bradley was now standing still with her arms out wide, twisting from left to right in a semicircle.

"Well, Detective? What do you mean?"

"Well, what the fuck do you think I mean, you morgue trash bandits. Where is my fucking corpse?"

Luis and Ramón looked around in stupefied silence.

"She's in the basement." Boomed a voice from the kitchen.

"Ah, Captain Merrick-a," Bradley exclaimed, softening the a at the end, followed by an eye roll from the captain, who was in no mood for Bradley's BS this morning.

"The victim, a Mrs. Audry Dearborn, a 64-year-old executive who worked at Bank of America and loved fine food and the theater is in the basement. In the trash room, to be more specific. I'm thinking that she was somehow suspended from the trash door, and the trash from apartments above piled up on her until the thin rope tied to her leg gave way, and the whole lot came down at once."

"And what brings you to this bewilderingly specific conclusion, Captain?"

"Well, Bradley, not that I am any match for your prodigious skill and experience—totaling an impressive three-year stretch of alcohol-fueled crime fighting—but I employed my humble detective skills that I've managed to cobble together over 38 years and noticed the rope around her foot, the 19 bags of trash laying atop the body, and this frayed rope tied to the handle of the trash door over here which appears to have about 140-pound breaking strain. The victim weighs around 140 pounds, in my estimation, which means, as trash built up on top of her, it was only a matter of time before the tether gave way and she fell to her death. I assume she was unconscious the whole time, but we won't know until the autopsy if she was already dead. Either way, she was not yelling out because it would be very loud through all the apartments below and above as the trash chute is in the middle of all the apartments in this line."

"Impressive. Why did you call me?"

"You entertain me, Bradley!"

He walked over toward the entry door to head for the basement but stopped when he realized she was serious, and he turned around for another shot.

"It's your damn job, Detective. Thanks to the early demise of your former superior officer and my lack of ability—despite my extensive attempts—to replace him. You are our acting chief homicide investigator. What do you mean, why did I call you?"

"I'm just saying, you seem to have this already wrapped up, Captain."

"Do me a favor, Detective; try to dazzle me by poking holes in my synopsis. It may be difficult because the victim no longer has a head. But dazzle away."

Luis and Ramón volunteered to take another elevator with the gurney, and they were very happy to have that excuse rather than risk upsetting the volatile Detective again. Bradley and Merrick shared an uncomfortable ride for eleven floors to the basement.

"Why did you ask me and the EMTs to meet you on the 10th floor if the body is in the basement?" Bradley asked to break the awkward silence.

"The crime scene is on the 10th floor. The basement is just where the body landed. I imagine he used this rope as a time delay strategy so that he would not be noticed leaving the scene at the time of the murder. I am not sure why the medics were up there, though. The doorman probably sent them up because that's where I went thirty minutes earlier."

The basement door opened, and the trash room was right across the way. There was blood pooling out of the trash room door that had seeped underneath all the trash bags lying on top of the body. It was a stinking mess of a murder scene, and Bradley was still far from form. The rancid trash combined with the rusty iron smell of the blood was starting to get to her.

"Well, there's not much we can find out here that the autopsy won't tell us. I suggest we go back upstairs and work the room a little. By the way, why did you assume the time delay?"

"Mrs. Lander up in 11C had been hearing the trash come down all day and land just below her apartment. She hardly hears the trash when it comes down at all, so she found this strange. She opened up the trash chute to take a look, and she could see the bags piling up only a foot down. Another bag dropped right at that second, scaring the living hell out of Mrs. Lander.

Then, all the bags dropped to the basement, and she heard it all land with a massive thud. So hard that it broke the trash compacter and spilled out onto the floor as you saw."

"And you've been here for how long?"

"Just 30 minutes, but it's amazing what you can get done with a clear head."

"Hmmm. I'm sure," Bradley harrumphed with disdain. "Was there anything in the trash that looked suspicious? A mask, perhaps?"

"I didn't look in the trash. What kind of murderer uses the trash can? Plus, I didn't want to deprive you of the pleasure—knowing your affinity for trash."

Merrick was referring to Bradley's string of distasteful suitors, and Bradley knew exactly what he implied.

"Yes, well, we can't all have little Miss Perfect at home, can we?"

Bradley was referring to Merrick's recent end to a 30-year marriage. The wound was still fresh, and Bradley's remark was just mean and cut deeply.

These two really hated each other, but they also somehow enjoyed each other's broken company. Codependent, damaged cops.

They got back up to 10C, and Bradley stomped open the trash.

"Nope. No such luck with the trash, Cap. I think this guy is turning up at the door; they're expecting him; he is probably wearing a mask, so he's not ID'd on security cams, and he's asking them to wear a mask, which he douses in sleepy juice, so he can execute them undisturbed."

"Okay, interesting, but where is her mask, and why would the victim agree to put on a mask for someone who just turned up at their door? I mean, it's not like we're in a pandemic anymore. That was two years ago. Nobody's wearing masks anymore."

"I'd say the mask could be at the bottom of that chute under the flesh' n trash pile, so we will need to inventory the trash that is not still bagged. As to why they'd comply with the request to put on a mask, maybe this guy has arranged to meet them and tells them he's immunocompromised. Art consultant, maybe."

"But how is he getting in and out undetected?"

"Well, considering the hanger in the trash chute was a time delay tactic, maybe he is coming and going out of time. We're not looking at the right times. He could get access hours or days before and be holed up in an empty apartment."

"But to have access like that in multiple buildings, he'd need to have access via building management or security."

"Not if he was a real estate broker."

"Not bad, Bradley. I knew there must be a reason I put up with you. So, we're looking for a male real estate broker who represents people wanting to buy property!"

"Maybe. I think there is a lot more to it than that, though. Let's take a look at the footage a day or two before and see who we can see."

They took the security footage on a flash drive and organized to also get the footage from the Apthorp.

Bradley didn't like the station much. Mainly because it was full of law enforcement officers which she didn't really care for. She opted instead to work from home whenever possible; much harder for the assholes to annoy you.

She poured herself a brittle. That's a gin and tonic with vodka instead of tonic. There's a stiff drink, and then there's a brittle. Sitting down to scour the security footage on her laptop, she flicked on the flatscreen on the wall. She found it easier to concentrate if she entertained her subconscious with movies that she had seen before but didn't have to pay attention to them. That left her conscious mind free to focus and stopped it from wandering. She looked at it as keeping the CPU busy, so it didn't have time to start imagining things. She watched all movement for two days before each murder and found nothing suspicious. Nobody entering with masks. Nobody entering that could not be easily identified. *This guy was a ghost,* she thought to herself.

* * *

Bradley's phone rang. Usually, she didn't answer calls, preferring to just call people back, but this was Rico. A young man she'd been seeing for tension relief.

They had met on the Staten Island Ferry after she'd been investigating a murder over there. Usually, murders on Staten Island were either related to the concrete business or the waste management business, but this was a little different. This was an old lady with no ties to anything or anyone aside from lawn bowls and cucumber sandwiches. She was discovered by a package deliverer days after her murder. The UPS driver said he saw something strange in the window and called the police. She was hanging from a rope that was connected to the ceiling fan, which had been left on. It was made to look like she had suicided by turning on the fan, which would twist up the rope enough to lift her off the floor and cut off her oxygen, but when the rope was fully extended, there was no way she could reach the ceiling fan switch. Of course, she could turn the fan on and run over and slip the noose around her neck, but Bradley smelled a rat. It just made no sense that she would kill herself. Bradley had thought about it being her guy practicing, but it was not the same type of thought process, not the same type of property—a single-family home instead of an apartment building—and it was not bizarre enough to be the same guy.

After leaving the scene, she decided to ride the ferry instead of sitting in the car with other detectives. She had just procured herself a Kahlua coffee. Booze that smelled like coffee would surely be a good cover. She walked to the top deck to take in the sunshine, and there, with his face in the wind and his eyes closed, was Rico. He could have been a polo player or a pool boy, and Bradley liked that about him. Unpretentious, handsome enough, rugged enough, she could play with this one for a while.

"Hey mamma, qué pasa?"

"Rico, if you want between these legs again, you'll quit it with the mamma, okay?"

"Okay, mamma. I mean princess."

"Better! You coming over?"

"I can come."

Bradley awoke to the screaming fucking blender which Rico was using to obliterate ice for his morning smoothy.

"What the actual fuck, Rico?"

"Sorry, mamma, I gotta go. These apartments won't sell themselves."

"You're a broker?"

"As of Monday, yes. See you mamacita, I'll call you."

For a fleeting moment, the idea went through her head, but she quickly disregarded it. Nobody who calls their hookup "mamacita" is capable of lunch-wrapping a chick to death.

She leapt out of bed in the way that she didn't every morning; by throwing a leg over the side like she was escaping from prison and slowly standing up. She was feeling slightly optimistic, but she knew if she could get some caffeine in her bloodstream, she'd soon come to her senses.

It was autopsy day, and Bradley was interested to see what they might find. As Captain Merrick had so aptly put it, *much harder without a head,* Bradley thought to herself. She drove downtown to the medical examiner's office only to find she was at the wrong one. There are four in Manhattan and eleven across the five boroughs, but the one that the murders usually go to was apparently out of action due to an outbreak of Legionnaires' disease from the HVAC system, and the whole building was shut down.

Bradley finally walked into the correct location an hour late, and Merrick was there glaring at her.

"Nice punctuality, Bradley. You missed the whole thing."

"A heads up on the location change would have been nice. And why are you here? Don't you have a department to run?"

"Let's just say I have a vested interest in the outcome of this case. Plus, you don't overwhelm me with trust."

"Well, I can't miss you if you won't leave. What's the verdict on 10C?"

"Her name is Patricia Bloom, as you well know, and she had zero trace of trihalomethane or any other sedative. The team did find gaff tape among the remains, and it looks like she was gagged with it, which would explain why nobody heard any yelling. I guess this guy just overpowered her, but she still must have known him to open the door. She also has several bruises, but it is impossible to tell what was from the fall and what was from any altercation."

"Okay, so how do we know it is even the same guy? Aside from the bizarre nature of the murders, there is nothing that actually ties them together."

"It is the randomness that is common. This guy is a creative. Maybe a writer. A real estate broker who's a writer, and he's got some crazy method-writer scenarios he likes to play out for his plots. I don't know, but I think this is our guy on both of these."

"Okay, so what now, Cap. Sit back and wait for another one. We don't have a single thing to follow."

"I guess so, Bradley, unless you dig something up."

That evening, Madeline Bradley sat afront a roaring February fire in her New York apartment and drank a bottle of cognac while she considered every possible angle of this peculiar psychotic creature and came up with not one inkling. She drifted off into a coma, dreaming of the next grotesque taking of a life and what demented tricks and traps he may have in store.

Hastings-on-Hudson

Peter J. Hastings sat in a wine bar on a Sunday afternoon on the Hudson River. An opulent fellow with a degree in English literature and a vocation that nobody could quite pin down. He disguised it neatly with the opaque veil of an executive search facilitator. That meant he could fly anywhere in the world under the assumption he was seeking top talent in the farthest of locations.

The truth was something far more sinister, or at least it would seem so from some of the nefarious or dangerous regions requiring a clandestine shroud. He was either a spy or a strategic advisor to those in a position to manipulate entire countries.

He started in the insurance business and found his niche negotiating with a Russian extortionist who kidnapped a corporate executive from his company. It became almost routine that when receiving a call stating, "I have your senior vice president of claims in the trunk of my car," then a $20,000 payment would be organized for the exchange. The greatest cover, of course, was simply that nobody would really believe them. The good old normalcy bias. "We live in America, and that type of nonsense doesn't go on here." But it did, and more often than anybody would ever believe. Nobody wanted anybody to die because then the game was over, and the landscape would change, so it was all kept very neat and tidy, organized via fax machines, and executed via bank wires hidden in plain sight as insurance claims.

Peter's James Bondesque mystique most certainly attracted the ladies of a certain type. Usually tall, brunette, Jewish, and would not look at all out of place in a Victoria's Secret catalog. They were always far younger than him, but a little mysterious charm, a handmade Bugatti sports car, and a black American Express card go a long way up a leg.

But today, Peter sat by himself. Not for any particular reason. He could make a phone call, and any one of seven princesses with questionable intentions would join him, but today he was just enjoying his solitude. He sensed a foreboding week ahead and strategically took the time to calm himself before the storm. Not that he was aware of any daunting activities, but after forty-five years of anticipating, one does tend to get a nose for bumpy weather.

He sipped his crisp Tokaji ice wine. Even though it was cold outside in New York in February on the river, today was sunny. So much so that you'd swear it was summer until you stepped outside to the threat of death by exposure.

Peter pondered his recent exploits, navigating the purchase of companies for his clients, firing teams of people who'd gotten complacent and needed a shakeup only to be hired back into different positions a week or two later. This real client work kept a tight lid on his other exploits that he never talked about. Not with anyone. Not even his closest friends. Which probably meant the Department of Defense or some powerful organization with its own geopolitical agenda. He had even worked on the Donald Trump election campaign prior to the 2016 election simply because his certain set of skills commanded a certain number of zeros in his fee, and he didn't particularly mind where the money came from; until he did.

Peter chose to live in Hastings-on-Hudson—a small village just up the Hudson River from Manhattan—because his last name gave an heir of ownership of the whole town.

Peter was startled out of a deep meditative trance by his phone ringing.

"Go for Hastings." He'd recently seen someone in a film answer a phone like this and decided to try it out.

"Peter, it's Madeline. Yes, Bradley. I'm fine, but I need your help. I'm in a bit of a spot with a case."

"A case? What the fuck are you talking about. You're a real estate developer."

"Well, yes, I was, but you know that thing with the mortgage litigation mess derailed me somewhat, and I had to, let's say, pivot. So now I'm working as a homicide detective here in the city."

"Fuck me," he exclaimed with genuine bewilderment.

"No, dear, those days are well behind us, I'm afraid, but I do miss your witty company and your vulgar vocabulary. Listen, can we meet?"

"Sure. I'm at my place on the river. You remember where?"

"Do I remember where? I built the fucking place,
you Muppet. I'll be there in forty minutes."

"I'll order your usual."

Bradley hit the basement in her private elevator, feeling
very much like Bruce Wayne hitting the Bat Cave. She
rocked up the West Side Highway and got to Hastings-
on-Hudson in 18 minutes. She walked into the restaurant on the water that her construction company had
built some years earlier and, as if he'd always been
there, Peter J. Hastings was sitting at his full window
table facing the Hudson River, with sunlight streaming
through onto his weathered skin softened slightly by
his cashmere turtleneck sweater.

"It's been a minute, ol' boy."

"Madeline, my dear. Or should I say, Detective?
I'm not sure I'll ever get used to that. So, what's
up with this 'case' you mentioned."

"Okay, so here's what's what…"

Bradley unfolded the whole story, the details of each
murder, and everything she'd pieced together so far,
which wasn't that much.

"Interesting. Okay. So why me, Bradley? I'm
sure you've got something very specific in mind
to make you reach out to me."

"Not really, no. I'm at a dead end on this and
if there is anyone I know that can get into the

head of someone just having their professional background and some behavioral traits, it's you. I've seen you decode people down to the bone, having heard their opening sentence and taken a peek at their shoes. Who am I looking for here?"

"Hmm. Well, you're right; he works in real estate because that gives him access to people and to properties, but he only works in real estate for that purpose. It's not his profession. He does something far more pragmatic. Measured. Certainly artistic. Perhaps a gallery owner with a real estate license. Come to think of it, art gives him the same, if not better, access to people, but not to buildings necessarily, so a combination of both makes sense. But there is more to him than that. I think he was a victim of human trafficking. Possibly even trafficked by his parents. That's the level of abandonment that drives a person to acts as inhumane and maniacal as these. I also think he'd be really fun company. A hedonistic sociopath with a penchant for overindulgence but keeping it well within his control. He'd never give up control."

"Out fucking standing. Do you have his address?"

Peter laughed and then smiled knowingly while staring back out into the river.

"No, but I'd probably recruit him to run something big. Maybe NASA. Somebody like this could easily manage a space program."

Hastings was half joking, but the fact was that most high-performing CEOs sported an almost identical profile. They just skipped a few steps along the way that would have led them to murderous deeds. Betrayal by a parent being the number one contender in the race to the bottom.

Bradley sat in silence, feeling like there was more to come. One little snippet that might give her an onramp to anything. Some place to point her silver Range Rover.

"Do you know what? I have a friend you may want to talk to in Cambridge. She's a professor at Harvard and has been there for decades. Somebody like this would stand out to her, and she just may have run across him, even if he didn't attend Harvard. People at that level tend to run across each other's paths. Her name is Johanna Mayor. I'll call her and let her know you are coming if you'd like."

"Perfect. Thank you, dear. You're a gentleman. As well as a depraved teenager."

"Ah, you know me so well. I'll text you the details for Johanna."

Bradley acknowledged with a slap on Peter's shoulder as she sprung to her feet and made her way to the exit. It was almost exactly a four-hour drive to Cambridge, and she would stay up there and seek out the professor in the morning.

Bradley could probably achieve the same thing on the phone, but something told her this was going somewhere. She felt compelled to meet in person.

Murder Three

Sunday evenings were a sacred time for Dr. Alexai Freeman. He loved his solitude, his books, and his fireplace. "The mind needs space and silence to work its magic," he would say to his private students. He especially loved his young female students and took great pleasure in heaping attention on them.

Alexai was in his mid-fifties but had developed a quiet, handsome strength and had recently discovered that young women found him mysterious and attractive, a surprising development that he found intriguing and also exciting.

Alexai had studied art history at Stanford and had nurtured a global following for his work as an author in the space. He had gotten lucky early in his career when he unwittingly discovered a multi-hundred-million-dollar art forgery underworld when he noticed an anomaly in the signature on a Kandinsky. It appeared to have been spelled with a C instead of a K. In reality, no such error had been made by the forger, but the downstroke of the K had been thin and, with a decade of age, had disappeared into the surrounding paint, leaving the odd-shaped "C" of Kandinsky's signature. Unfortunately for the crime syndicate, the discovery led to an investigation that focused on this forger's style, which then uncovered an inconsistency in the materials used. It was a subtle chemical inaccuracy in the production of red ochre that could only be reproduced using Russian yellow ochre that was heated to become red. There was no way to reproduce it without the original ochre, and African ochre had been used, which matches perfectly in color but not chemical composition.

Alexai's credit for the discovery put him on the map and gave him high authority in the art world as a private tutor.

This Sunday was different from the others as he had allowed for a private session. He never would sacrifice the solace of his sacred evening, but this was a particularly attractive and seductive young lady, and she only had Sunday available in her schedule.

As the 9:00 PM chime sounded on Dr. Freeman's Ridgeway grandfather clock—the last chime of the evening as Ridgeway had introduced the first nighttime silence mechanism for their clocks in 1930—the doorbell rang.

Alexai opened the door with comedic vigor.

"Good evening, my dear."

"Hi, professor. Thank you so much for taking the session on a Sunday for me. I really appreciate it."

"Of course, Talia. I'm happy to accommodate you."

Talia Nistratov, the daughter of Alexander Nistratov—a Russian on the lam after a government-level real estate fraud in Moscow that netted him $150MM—was a rare beauty, but tonight, Alexai was particularly aroused by her firm young body tightly wrapped in a sheer velvet green dress.

Talia noticed him staring, and it was beginning to make her uncomfortable.

* * *

Bradley arrived in Boston. It was 9:30 PM, and she was tired after hitting traffic that had extended her drive time to 7 hours. She checked into a Hilton and went directly to Boston Chops Steakhouse. She had called Dr. Mayor at Harvard from the car and arranged to meet first thing in the morning. Bradley's "first thing" and Dr. Mayor's were vastly different, but she agreed that 6:30 for breakfast was a reasonable hour despite her horror at the thought.

She ordered a bourbon and a New York strip, then sat in quiet contemplation about it all. Having already downed two double Bullet bourbons, she ordered a third as her steak came out. Smothered in bourbon peppercorn sauce, she wolved down the steak like it was her last meal and washed it down with the Bullet. Now in a foggy bourbon haze, Bradley meandered back to her lodgings and fell swiftly into her comfortable coma until the alarm brought her back around at 6:00 AM.

She showered quickly and scurried downstairs to retrieve her car from the parking lot. As she was driving over to meet Dr. Mayor, her phone rang. It was Captain America.

"Captain!"

"Bradley, how soon can you be down at 200 Riverside Boulevard?"

"In about six hours."

"What the…"

"Calm down! I'm up in Cambridge following a lead with a Harvard professor. I can leave in an hour, and it's a four to five-hour drive. Why, what's up."

"There's been another murder. A double. An art history professor, Alexai Freeman, and his lover, Talia Nistratov."

"Hmmm. Does it seem like our guy?"

"I have no idea, Bradley. Believe it or not, I can't always be on the scene doing your job for you. Just get there as soon as you can."

She hung up the phone as she pulled into the Harvard campus. "Pahk ya cah in the Hahvid yahd," she murmured to herself as she pulled up and stepped out. Dr. Mayor was already there waiting for her to go to breakfast.

"Pleased to meet you, professor. Thank you for meeting me."

"Not at all, Detective. Happy to help, and any friend of Peter Hastings is bound to be interesting."

"Indeed. Unfortunately, I've been called back to the city as there has been another incident, so I don't have much time."

"No problem, let's go eat, and we will talk on the way."

They both walked across the street to a little coffee shop off Harvard Square and took a table outside.

"I've been thinking about what you said on the phone, Detective, and the description actually fits a few people that I have come across, but there is one that comes to mind that gave me quite the bone-chilling shiver when I thought about him in context with these horrible murders. I don't even know why. I never considered him in this light before, but I woke up at 3:00 AM with a shock like it had come to me in my sleep. I had thought deeply about the description you gave me and obviously carried it into my dreams.

Many years ago, I attended an art history convention hosted by Stanford. It was the usual old fair, blowhards extolling their wisdom for hours with an interesting point every hour or two. I was sitting next to a young gentleman who kept staring at me. He was a very attractive young man in his twenties, and I was far younger then, probably in my late thirties. We struck up a conversation, and before we knew it, we were out having a drink.

He was absolutely brilliant. I'd never heard anyone speak so intuitively about so many subjects. He was very well-traveled, and his art history knowledge was intriguing to me for somebody so young. We went out for coffee and then drinks and spent the whole afternoon together. At the end of the day, we said goodbye, and he asked me if he could come by my hotel room the next day and show me a piece that he had procured. As much as I liked him and respected his incredible knowledge, I declined. I told him I was taking the day to write, and I'd be in total lockdown. 'Perfect,' he said. I looked at him, thinking it was a strange comment. 'The perfect situation for a writer.' He said, seeming to correct himself."

"So, what's strange about that?" Bradley said, now completely absorbed in her story.

"The next day at 1 PM, there was a knock at my door at Hotel Nikko up in the city. I'd been staying down near Stanford but wanted a few days in San Francisco before I left town. It was him. He had a look on his face that terrified me. I had not told him I was going to stay at the Nikko, so it immediately seemed strange, and it all hit me quickly when I saw that look on his face. He was about to walk in, and I began walking back when, right at that moment, a waiter with my room service order wheeled the tray right up behind him. He turned around, and his whole demeanor changed."

"What did he do?"

"He just apologized and said, 'I see I have come at a bad time. I'll be sure to call ahead in the future.' I just glared at him to make sure he knew that I knew. Over the years, I forgot about the incident entirely, but your call brought it all flooding back."

"And do we have a name for this mysterious murdery brainiac?"

"Yes, his name was Darby. Darby Finn. I monitored his name via academic channels for years, but nothing ever came of it. He just vanished. For all I know, he wasn't Darby Finn to start with. I never saw him again. Thank God. And I certainly hope that won't change. But he fits your profile. He could morph into anyone with charm and wit, but that underlying evil is ever present. I'm sure of it."

Bradley thanked Professor Mayor and got on the road back to the city.

Of course, there was nothing to actually link this guy to any of it, she thought to herself. *It's just one person's coincidental link, but the professor seemed so certain of it—I can't let it go.*

Bradley often had these conversations with herself. Like there were two people inside her head going back and forth, it helped give the conversation structure like she had someone else in the car with her. Either that or an undiagnosed disorder. She was comfortable with either.

She tore recklessly down the Henry Hudson Parkway in record time and was back on the West Side in three and a half hours. She pulled up at 200 Riverside Boulevard and parked untidily out front. She liked to do that as it looked all "official police business" while saving the time it took to park properly. Decades of receiving parking tickets outside her Manhattan construction projects had built up to crisis level, and the relief of parking no longer being a burden was like getting out of jail free.

Bradley walked into the lobby and spoke to the people at the front desk, who were in quite a state, wondering why it had taken so long for homicide to arrive. Bradley disregarded their concern entirely with another flippant comment.

> "So, there's a body or two lying about that need attention, I'm told."

The shocked young female concierge held her tongue, led Bradley to the elevator, and pushed 33.

> "33E Detective. Forgive me if I don't accompany you."

> "Imagine my regret," Bradley said, half under her breath but loud enough to land.

She walked into 33E calmly and casually, not knowing quite what to expect. There were two uniforms in the kitchen cooking pop tarts. Bradley nodded at them knowingly.

> "Pop Tart detective?"

> "No. Thank you. I'm no longer fucking seven. And this is a murder scene if I'm not mistaken.

Oh, fuck it. You know what? I'm so hungry I could eat a human liver. Give me one of those fucking things."

Bradley strolled on through the house, munching on her pop tart, and looked back over her shoulder to the officers with a mouth full, nodding her appreciation and saluting with her pop tart.

"She's quite the baller!" whispered one officer to the other.

"Thank you," came Bradley's voice from the other room while the cops looked at each other with surprise.

Bradley walked into the bathroom to see Mr. Freeman and Ms. Nistratov in the shower naked. She was leaning against the glass at a 45-degree angle with her legs spread, and he was standing between her legs on the opposite angle with his back facing against the wall, so the pair were in a V, which looked impossible at first to Bradley until she looked at the mechanics. Freeman was suspended by the metal shower hose that was wrapped around his waist and tied off, and she was being held up by him as if in a bizarre sexual pose. Right at that second, the shower hose gave way, and the entire human sex sculpture came crashing down in a heap of skin and blood. *Not a lot of blood*, Bradley thought.

She wondered if the blood had been drained from their bodies and washed down the drain, but she didn't know enough about biology, science, or anatomy yet, so she'd have to wait for an autopsy. *But they certainly did not look well,* she mused internally, as she often did to entertain herself.

The uniform cops came in behind her, wondering what the hell was going on.

"Well, that scared the living fucking shit out of me," said Bradley with honest and justified shock on her face.

"What did you do?" asked one of the officers.

"Well, imagine this. I was standing here examining the scene, and I brought the whole thing down with my mind. What the fuck do you think I did? Wait a minute. Have you not been in here yet?"

"No, ma'am. Officer Luis told us not to go in, or you'd have our balls. Literally."

"Yes, Luis is a much smarter man than he used to be."

"Yes, ma'am."

"Don't fucking call me ma'am, dude. That is a contraction of madam. Do I look like I own a fucking brothel? Actually, don't answer that if you value your stones."

"No, detective."

"So, nobody photographed this artwork before it came crashing down? Maybe that toity little bitch in the lobby."

Just then, the coroner's office arrived with a gurney.

"Hello, Harry. I bet you weren't expecting to see me so soon."

"Detective Bradley. Actually, whenever I think of death, I think of you."

"Touché, you fat bastard but the amount you think about death, you must be thinking about me all the fucking time. Makes me warm and tingly just thinking about it. Now, down to business. These two were strung up like Cirque du Soleil in this artful pornographic installation until the shower hose suspending them broke, and they both came—simultaneously—crashing down."

"Did you get a picture," said Harry.

"Sadly, no! I wasn't aware of any time constraints and was just analyzing the mastery of art and engineering when boom. Death spaghetti."

"Hmm. Death spaghetti. Lovely. I see your way with words has not diminished in either depravity or depth of description."

"Well, we do what we can for the literary appreciative, Harry. I'll go down and see if I can get a photograph from that Gen Z in the lobby. I'm sure she took one. She had that little dismissive 'know it all' quality about her."

As Bradley was about to walk out, Gen Z walked in.

> "Oh, good, I was just coming to find you. Actually, I will take a look at that photograph you took," said Bradley while yanking the phone out of her hand to the absolute shock of the 23-year-old concierge.

> "What? I didn't. Give me back my…"

> "Aha, here it is. I see you are already sharing it on your private little text group here. That's a fuck load of OMGs all in a row, I must say, Bianca. I see your name is Bianca. Can I call you Bianca? Of course I can; it's your fucking name, isn't it! You do understand this is a crime scene that you've corrupted, and you'll obviously have to go to prison?"

All this was hitting Bianca like a hail of bullets, and she was still in that dazed state where you don't quite know how to respond.

> "Don't fucking worry about it, dear. I'm just fucking with you because people your age make me piss blood, but I do appreciate you offering up the photo. That is very helpful."

> "Oh, You're very welcome. Happy to help."

> "What are you doing here, Bianca?"

> "Oh, I forgot, there's a fire truck downstairs that cannot get past a silver Range Rover because it is parked, blocking one and a half lanes."

"And is there a fire?"

"I'm not sure."

"Okay, here's the keys. Just move it out and put it back when they leave."

"But I can't."

"Bianca. Are you or are you not a concierge?"

"Yes, but I can't drive."

"Well then, don't crash it because it's a police car, and you'll be in deeper shit than you're already in. Go!, go!"

Bianca looked around the room at the coroner and the cops for some sort of direction. The cops motioned for her to leave and made the "she's nuts" head circles with their fingers.

Bradley looked at the photo that she had already texted to herself and noticed that the shower hose was not tied but connected by some sort of thin white tie. She went over to the shower and picked up the shower hose to see it was a long white cable tie, but it didn't look like it snapped; rather, it had been burned.

She started looking around for what might have caused this, and she noticed a little white button object stuck to the white tile. It looked like a little motion sensor. She photographed it and then pulled it off the wall. It was a tiny camera, and it looked like it might be connected to the Wi-Fi system. *This bastard was watching,* Bradley thought to herself. She kept looking around on the shower floor and noticed a small silver device. She picked it up and smelled it. It was an explosive of some type. A mini charge—enough to sever the cable tie and triggered by a detonator that must have also been connected to the Wi-Fi. This was a whole new level. It was now interactive. She looked down into the little white camera and smiled. Not a friendly smile. More like a psychotic teeth-gnashing nod.

Bradley bagged up the evidence and left. Now, she was more intrigued than ever. She was also pissed because she now knew that she was being played with. Possibly directly targeted. Which meant this is about to get interesting.

On the drive back to the station, Bradley started thinking back to the other scenes. Could she have missed anything? Were there tiny cameras in those murders, and she just overlooked them? *Of course, there were. Why wouldn't there be? This guy is fucking with me,* Bradley thought to herself while getting angrier and angrier.

She got to the station and went to see Baggs in evidence. She had no idea what his name was; she just called him Baggs because that's who she gave her evidence bags to.

"Yo, Baggs. That scene at the Apthorp and the one at Park Ave. Do you think you could have it scanned again and look for some additional items?"

"Bradley, my name is Kevin. Kevin Briggs."

"Well, I knew it had a B in it. That's progress, right?"

"No!"

"So! The evidence?"

"Oh, let me just hop right up and check."

"Yes, very kind. I'm looking for these little stick-on WIFI cameras on any surfaces." Bradley threw the device to him inside an evidence bag. "Call me when you have some answers. Oh, and log that for me, would you?"

"You're a piece of work, Bradley."

"Yes, thank you!"

Bradley Finny

Madeline Bradley was heading home but was lured mysteriously by the call of her local bar; her favorite place to think. It was the library bar at the Hudson Hotel on West 59th. Naturally, she parked right out the front, where there was absolutely no parking. The doorman, who knew Bradley very well, casually quipped while she alighted the vehicle and walked by.

"Another murder upstairs no doubt, Detective!"

"You know me so well, Dennis."

"It's David."

Bradley responded with her usual respectful retort which was to not even acknowledge that he'd spoken.

As she nursed her bourbon in a deep leather chair in front of the fireless fireplace, she dwelled on the idea that this guy was singling her out and playing with her. But why? Could it be somebody she had met? Somebody she had wronged. Somebody she had slept with. Somebody she had not slept with. The possibilities made her head spin; with a little help from the bourbon, now her third.

The search for Darby Finn had turned up nothing. There was just no such person in police records, academia, art, or real estate. In fact, there was only one person in the world named Darby Finn, and it was an Irish girl. There was something about the name Finn that was familiar to Bradley, though. Somebody she had met. *What was that guy's name in Puerto Vallarta, Mexico, that I met at the resort pool bar? It must have been a decade ago. Finny. Bradley Finny, that was it because we laughed about having the same name.*

Bradley was now deep in thought but didn't feel like she was getting anywhere. Just dredging up old memories with no relevance to the case. But it continued to play on her mind because Bradley Finny certainly stood out to her at the time.

He was very smooth and sophisticated. She remembered wondering at the time why this guy was at a couples' resort alone, but then again, she was at a couples' resort alone. She often did this when vacationing as there was less chance of being plagued by pickup lines like at singles places. She had no patience for it, and if anyone was doing the picking up, it was her—when she felt like it.

The more she thought about it, the more that came back to her. She recalled that she was very rude to him for trying to speak with her but after the initial collision, she let down her guard as he was less pathetic than most of her pursuers. The conversation was surprisingly in-depth, and she opened far more than ever. He seemed to have a powerful grasp on influence, much like a psychologist.

She was still a real estate developer back then and was constantly on the lookout for investors, which is another reason she had let her guard down. He seemed very interested in her vocation. He was the first person who thought she would make a good detective. In fact, when they were playing the "what do you do" guessing game, his first guess was a police detective, and her first guess for him was art dealer.

This was starting to look more and more interesting. She wrote down his name in her notebook—partly because it seemed oddly relevant and partly because she remembered him fondly—and continued to reminisce. It was not a hot, heavy romance. It wasn't even a romance. It was more of an intellectual stimulation. They spent the whole evening together, drank, ate, talked, and laughed. The hours just flew away—dissolved by drinks, cocaine, and cigarettes—and before they knew it, the sun was rising; they had talked all night. It was like he had known her for years, her every thought, hope, and dream. They spoke with the fluidity and familiarity of old friends with a history.

Bradley woke up mid-morning in the pool cabana alone. He was gone. Just a note saying: "It was a beautiful night; we'll meet again if and when the planets align. Had to fly, Brad."

Her mind was foggy. Her coke and bourbon hangover weighed heavy, and all the miles they covered in their all-night conversations seemed like a blur. She felt fulfilled and truly sated, even though there was not even a kiss, let alone sex.

Murder Four

Bradley didn't even remember coming home from the Hudson. But she had obviously been in a playful mood because Rico was laying in the bed next to her, and judging by the state of the room, the bed, and herself, there had been some action. Her breath tasted like cigars, so no doubt she had gone to the Carnegie Club for one of her late-night nightcaps, which often turned into a Rico encounter.

She was in no mood for communicating, so she let him sleep and slipped out quietly to shower and get into the day. She was feeling oddly optimistic. Perhaps her reminiscing about that wonderful night had set her on a happier path, at least momentarily.

Her happy mindset was immediately shattered by a call from Captain America.

"Cap, sup? You got some deadies for me?"

"Do you think you'll ever take this job seriously, Bradley, or is this the way it's going to be?"

"Well, if we have to deal with death daily, don't you think it relieves the burden a little if we're ever so slightly not giving a fuck?"

"I don't know, maybe you're right and we're all wrong, Bradley. Crazier things have happened. Better get in your car and get over to Fort Lee. The Modern apartment complex."

"You want me to go to fucking Jersey. What the absolute fuck?"

"Well, it's your guy. The vic is hanging naked by the ankles from a window washing rig. Another resident got quite the good morning when he raised his blinds a half hour ago."

"Sounds thrilling. I'm on my way. By the way, what makes you think it's my guy?"

"Well, your name is written across her chest in lipstick."

"Madeline?"

"No, Bradley. Remember, you've got no jurisdiction over there, so you are a consulting detective. Do try not to embarrass the department. Or the state. Please!"

"You have nothing to fear, Cap. Think of me as Detective Diplomat."

"Oh fuck," said Merrick under his breath as he hung up the phone.

Bradley smiled to herself, knowing that Merrick was actually starting to like her in some strange, dysfunctional way. These were the sort of relationships that she liked. People who knew her well enough to just let her be and get on with it. Well, maybe that was the case, or maybe she was starting to like him in some strange, dysfunctional way. Either way, it was working for her.

Bradley saw the body hanging from the tower as she crossed the George Washington Bridge. She was on the east end of the south tower. The Modern has two towers, and if the body was hanging on the other sides, people would have been able to see the act in progress, but facing the Hudson River, there was nobody to see anything at night, and from the street, it was obscured by a terraced lower building that was attached.

Bradley was already running the scenario as she drove. She was hoping that this guy was not going to play the same game and let the body drop to the ground at the last minute, but that would not be like him. He doesn't seem to run the same gag twice, aside from the little cameras.

Pulling up at The Modern reception and lobby, Bradley was greeted by a team of Jersey police and detectives who seemed just thrilled to see her. She threw open her door with her super wide shit-eating grin and exuded friendliness with her between-the-lines fuck-you.

> "Detective Bradley. We understand from Captain America that we might be able to assist you by offering our expertise," said the six-foot-three detective Sam Whithers.

> "Hah. You call him that, too? You know he hates that, right?"

> "Yeah, we know! So, we're told you know this doer?"

"Apparently, he's leaving me personal messages now?"

"Perhaps so. Where would you like to start?"

"Let's go to the apartment where our girl is hanging out."

Detective Whithers shot a less-than-forgiving side eye to Bradley for her flippant comment. They made their way to the 28th floor of the east tower and entered apartment C.

There she was, in all her glory. Legs held apart by a baseball bat, each end gaff taped to her ankles. Arms dangling down. She was athletic and posed like an X. Right there on her chest under her breasts, written upside down so it now appeared right way up to read; BRADLEY written in lipstick.

Bradley was carefully surveying the walls for a tiny camera, but there was nothing.

"Where is the victim from, Detective," asked Bradley.

"Her name is Pamela Wheeler. 40C upstairs. She managed a gallery on Madison around the corner from the Marc Hotel over in your neck of the woods. It looks like she was taken to the roof alive. Maintenance is arriving now so we can bring the equipment up and inspect the body."

"How do you know she was taken up there alive?"

"At first, we saw no sign of struggle in her apartment, then we noticed she had a Ring camera on her front door. Her cell phone had no password protection, so we just opened the app to view the video.

At 1:00 AM this morning, Miss Wheeler came out of her apartment and was looking around for something. She was carrying a baseball bat. She did not look scared, but she did look defensive. I guess that is an odd time of night for unexpected visitors. Nobody called her phone, so we can only assume they were yelling something out to her. Unfortunately, these halls on each floor are not monitored, just the entrances and exits, and nobody unaccounted for was detected coming in or out for 24 hours before or since the homicide. After standing out here in a silk nightgown for 30 seconds, she walked off down the hall, and that was the last that anyone saw of her.

Once we know the time of death, we can start to piece the timeline together."

"Very smart, detective."

"I have the same camera at my house, so it was not a giant academic leap. But what is interesting is this doer obviously knew about the camera and somehow lured her out. You can move slowly around this system, and it won't detect motion, so he could have looked around the corner slowly, seen the Ring, and formed a plan. Or he knew about it in advance."

"Got it. Very interesting, Detective. Can we go up and have a look at this body and see what else we can discover?"

"Let's do it."

The team took the elevator to the roof, where the window cleaning system was now fully raised and was being brought in from the edge. The body of Pamela Wheeler hung almost still with the slight wind moving her gently. Bradley walked up to view the other side of the girl. On her back, again written upside down, was the word FIND.

Bradley wrote the words in her book. She liked lists. They led places. They formed ideas. They caused one to think from other directions, and she was a very visual person.

As the coroner came in to process the body, Bradley stared out across the river, thinking deeply. Her trance was interrupted abruptly by a flash of light from across the river on the other side of the George Washington Bridge. It immediately occurred to her that if there were no mini cameras at this scene, an alternative might be to monitor people up on a rooftop using a telescope. And that might explain the location of this murder. "If someone was watching, they'd have wanted us to be on the roof," said Bradley out loud.

"What was that, Detective?" Whithers asked with a surprised tone.

"Nothing," said Bradley. "Just thinking out loud. There is not a mark on this body, so what are we liking for cause of death?"

"There is a puncture mark in the bottom of her foot," said the coroner. "This could easily be an induced overdose of some kind. We will know more when we get the tox results. She was still alive when she was hung upside down, and there is residual glue around her mouth, indicating she was probably gagged with heavy tape to stop her screaming."

"How do you know she was alive when she was hung upside down?" asked Bradley.

"You see the deep cuts in her ankles where the ropes were wrapped? The depth of the lacerations would indicate a prolonged struggle. She was definitely trying to break free. He probably knocked her out with an agent, then tied her feet and used the lift to raise her up, then waited until she regained consciousness. Once he injected her with whatever killed her, probably fentanyl or something similar, he would have removed the gag and lowered her down."

"And why to the 28th floor," said Whithers.

"I bet it's because he knew the shades would be down. He's been surveilling the building to see who drops their shades and raises them with some regularity. He probably had a clear path down to the 28th," Bradley pontificated with some confidence.

"Well, let's go find out!" said Whithers.

They got back in the elevator and started going door to door in the C line which was the apartments in the east end of the south tower. Knocking on every door and asking residents about their shades took some time, but eventually, they got down to 27. Sure enough, everybody above was in the habit of lowering and raising their shades with the sun, but 27 was a young man who was unaffected by the moving of the light and dark of it, and they just stayed up all the time.

> "Well, you certainly missed out!" said Bradley with a wry smile, causing another deep "Are you fucking kidding me?" glare from Whithers. "Hey, do you mind if I have a look at your telescope?"

Bradley walked over and took command of the device. She was looking over at the Castle Houses up in Hudson Heights on the Manhattan side of the river. She was looking for where the flash of light might have come from.

> "What do you use this telescope for?" asked Bradley, already expecting a defensive answer.

> "Oh, you know, stars and other astrological wonders."

> "Mmhmmm, an astrologer. Yes, I can certainly see that," said Bradley in her most sarcastic tone.

Bradley froze. She was staring directly into another telescope with the figure of a man behind it. *Was it a rubber-necker trying to get a glimpse of the naked dead chick? Possibly so, but what a location for casing a scene like this,* Bradley thought to herself, standing up to see what she could recognize with the naked eye. Noting the apartment in the Castle Houses, she didn't tell Whithers what she was thinking. After all, it was back on her island and in her jurisdiction.

"Bradley, have you finished your astrological homework?" said Whithers with an impatient tone.

"Yes, all done here, Detective. Thank you for your indulgence, and thank you, young man, keep looking upwards. You never know what you might be confronted with if you point this thing below 60 degrees. Or maybe you do." Bradley smiled her naughty smile at the young man.

Riding down, Whithers started probing.

"So why Find Bradley and why the baseball bat between her ankles?"

"Well, I assume so that you would call me; this guy is starting to play some games. As for the bat, I think he's just entertaining himself. His victims and crime scenes all have some slightly comedic or absurd twist."

Bradley thanked Whithers by saying she was surprisingly unpissed-off with the whole affair.

"So nice to meet somebody I don't immediately despise, Whithers," she said with her own special brand of affection.

"Thank you, Bradley. I, too, was surprised by not wanting to immediately throw you off a building. From Captain America's pre-sell, I was expecting somebody far less intelligent."

"Well, now you're just being flowery and con-descending—unless you're being sarcastic. In which case I am far more comfortable."

"See ya, Bradley. Looking forward to our next opportunity to stand over some corpses."

"I'll count the hours."

Hmmf! They both thought to themselves. *Unusual!*

Bradley headed straight for the Castle Houses to see what it looked like from the other side. She knew that it was the floor under the penthouse and the second apartment in from the left in the second building up from the south tower.

Fanny Bird—Real Estate Investor

In 2007, just before the global financial crisis—which was about to hit those holding massive debt super hard—Bradley's real estate development business was in its usual constant swing between teetering on failure and rocking back to potential greatness. She was buying townhouses for eight million dollars and knocking them down which takes a very special brand of either stupidity or giant brass balls. Then, she would build back a lavish mansion and sell it for three times as much. Sometimes.

This, of course, always put her in the market for cash. Massive amounts of very expensive cash. It didn't really bother her because when she exited, profit was usually in the millions, so paying hundreds of thousands of dollars for short-term debt capital was just another tax deduction and cost of doing business.

Of course, to meet people with enough available cash and an appetite for risk, Bradley had to go to where they were, which was usually private islands owned by friends and other equally opulent destinations. Private jets, limousines, full-time staff, and lavish misbehavior. She fit right in.

One summer, Bradley was on a money safari in the British Virgin Islands where she had spent enough time to be very well known. The days were usually fairly well-behaved, with water sports, boating, parachuting, windsurfing, and helicopter shark fishing. Not that she was much for fishing, but she did find herself being drawn to the idea of casting a line from a chopper to see if she could hook a great white.

Nights, however, were out of control. Wastefully lavish wines with implausibly extravagant meals and criminally illicit drugs for those who partook. Everything was available, which usually led to excessive promiscuity. It was the type of location where nothing seemed surreal, and talking or sleeping with celebrities was just part of the fare. This particular evening, Bradley found herself engaged with and attracted to a young actor with the surname, well, let's leave that out.

When it came to pillow talk, Bradley was adept at turning the conversation to investment for whatever insanely expensive project she was working on at the time. Tonight was no different. It was easy for her because she'd just start talking about architecture or interior design and then flip into what she was thinking for her project. She had a way of making it sound so engaging and exciting that they'd feel stupid not getting involved. In Mr. new-man's case, he lit up at the prospect of investing in elite, New York, one-of-a-kind mansion development, but more importantly, he knew someone who had deep enough pockets to scale the business to a dozen projects at a time.

"You need my Fanny, he said."

"Darling," Bradley said in her best Mae West tone, "it was your fanny that got us into this," slapping him on his backside.

"Yes, well, all other fannies aside, I have this investor who likes to put money into films. I've never met her in person, but she reached out to me via my manager, and, you know, my manager always lights up at the term 'film investment,' so my gatekeeper becomes the opposite, but I took the meeting. Her name is Fanny Bird. All our business is done on video calls, and she is quite the recluse, but she is always looking for ways to put more of her mountainous piles of cash to work, and I think she would love your development strategies."

"Well, wonderful." Bradley was already sliding out of bed, assuming that things could not possibly go any better than they had, and she'd gotten all she was going to get out of this interaction. "I've got to go to my bed before I do anything I'll regret."

"Well, I can't imagine what that might be considering what went down here."

"Yes, going down indeed. My point precisely. Toodle-oo. You were quite fabulous, you know."

Bradley exited the room to smiling applause for her graceful sweeping dip after slipping her LBD back on. *Dinner and a shag would have been a good enough evening,* she thought to herself, *but new investment put the other two to shame.*

The next morning, sure enough, there was a text message introducing her to Fanny Bird which was followed by an invitation to a video meeting.

After exhaustive internet research on the plane ride home, Bradley found absolutely nothing. Whoever Fanny Bird was, her privacy was intact. *More and more mysterious,* she thought to herself before ordering another stiff bourbon and soda—hold the soda.

The plane touched down at JFK, and Bradley lined up to get through customs with another five plane-loads of arrivals. Almost two hours later, she was finally through and making her way to the parking lot to retrieve her silver Range Rover just in time for her conference with Fanny. Bradley clicked the link to launch Skype on her brand-new Apple iPhone, which was released a few weeks earlier. The video launched to a shadowy silhouette with a raspy whispering voice. Bradley could hardly see her face, but she leapt right into her pitch bitch mode.

> "Ms. Bird, it is a pleasure to connect with you, and I'm excited to discuss possibilities regarding investment in my project."

> "Yes, yes," came the whispering rasp, almost too low to make out. "I've heard good things, but trust comes slowly to me." Bradley peeled off the Belt Parkway and pulled up in a side street, so she could fully focus on the conversation.

"I'm sorry, Ms. Bird, I was having trouble hearing, so I had to pull over."

"Call me Fanny, dear. I was saying that I don't trust you because I've never done business with you, and I've found in my long, lonely life that there is only one way to trust, and that is by results. I don't believe a word you're going to tell me; I'll only trust results, so I'm going to risk five million and not a penny more to give you an opportunity to prove yourself. Now, what can you do for me?"

"Well, I do have a prospective property on the Upper West Side that I can take down for seven million that will be worth twenty-two million after a gut renovation that will cost another five million, leaving us an eight-to-ten-million-dollar profit on sale. I can fund the construction with debt, so all I need is an additional two million to take down the deal."

"As I said, you've got five, so find out who you have to fuck to get another two, and we're off to the fucking races dear."

Bradley laughed. She liked this old girl.

"Ok, Fanny, I'll get to work."

"Yes, you will, dear. Send me the draft agreement and your wire details. Don't fuck this up, dear, will you!"

Bradley was about to say, "No, Ma'am," but the screen went blank. *Straight to the point,* Bradley thought. *That's refreshing.*

The next morning, Bradley flew into action and had the investment paperwork drafted up, giving a 50% equity share to her new investor, Fanny Bird Inc. The executed paperwork was returned immediately via email without a single redline or change of any kind. The wire followed within the hour, and Bradley got to work raising the capital she was short. She has one million in her operating account that she really needed to run her operation, but if she closed the construction funding fast enough, that would bridge the operating short. That meant she needed one more equity investor for a million dollars. She called the last three people who had invested with her who had all made a healthy return. She left messages with all three and waited for them to respond for the whole day. Meanwhile, she reached out to secure the property. It was going so perfectly that Bradley was having trouble believing it. All three investors had responded positively to the investment opportunity, so she gave each of them a 1/3 stake. She could have taken more, probably a million each but she would be reducing her own equity, and debt was always better than equity partners to preserve your own returns. Usually, she had to work much harder to get deals done, but it was a perfect storm of efficiencies. What she didn't know was that there was a far more ominous storm coming her way.

Murder Five

New York—Present day

The phone—still cupped in Bradley's hand from the night before, where she fell asleep in her over-stuffed lounge chair in a blurry bourbon haze—rang loudly and vibrated, shocking her awake.

"Bradley," Capt. Merrick announced in a tone, assuming she was hung over, "Wipe your drool, pour some coffee down your neck, and meet me downtown. I'll text you the address. He's struck again."

"Dad? Is that you? Why are you calling so early?"

"BRADLEY!"

"Yes, yes, Cap. I'm already up and out mowing my lawn. See you there."

"Lawn? Hello?"

Bradley was half joking and half drunk-dreaming, but she enjoyed taunting Captain America. Her phone buzzed as she stumbled out of the shower. The text said:

"910 Main St NY, NY."

"WTF is that?"

"The lighthouse on Roosevelt."

"Roosevelt Drive? FDR????"
"Roosevelt Island, damn it."

"Well, why don't you just fucking say Island."

"Do you not have a fucking GPS? I gave you the goddamn address. Sorry, I couldn't send a limo with an escort. Is it just me, or are you especially annoying today?"

"Just you!"

Getting to Roosevelt Island is something Bradley had never pondered. She only knew about the cable car, and she'd heard there was some bridge that you had to drive to Queens to get on. She asked her phone how to get to Roosevelt Island, and it said there was a subway. *A fucking subway?* She thought to herself. She really hated the subway. Being trapped underground every time some asshole jumped on the tracks to end it all. Another "incident on the tracks," as they liked to announce. The cable car was out of the question, and just fuck the subway. Driving was her only acceptable option. She knew that she was still way over the legal limit. Fortunately, she was a police officer.

It had snowed overnight, and traffic was even more unbearable than usual, but she had her trusty siren and portable flashing thing with a magnet to slap it on the roof. She loved that thing. Even with a siren and light the other drivers couldn't quite bring themselves to get out of the way in a timeframe that Bradley was comfortable with.

She roared up the Henry Hudson and flipped over to the East Side at the George Washington Bridge. All the way, she took the emergency shoulder wherever possible. She just loved blasting past the proles. She was making great time as she screamed around Randalls Island and over to Astoria where she could get access to the Roosevelt Island bridge.

Bradley was quite intrigued as she drove the bridge. To her right, she could see some activity up by the lighthouse. A large crowd of people had assembled. Bradley honked, and slowly, the crowd parted to let her through. She could not quite comprehend what she was seeing in front of her as the crowd parted. There seemed to be a head suspended between five bronze-sculptured faces. Bradley pulled up, got out, and headed over to investigate.

Four uniformed officers were holding back the line to keep the scene clean. Nobody else had arrived on the scene yet, so Bradley asked the uniforms what they knew.

> "It's a little bizarre, detective. The severed head has been suspended by these two steel wires. Looks like piano wire forming an X between these four heads. Then, in front of each face is a limb sticking out of the snow."

Bradley walked over, and sure enough, there was a leg sticking up out of the ground with the foot pointing back at the face. The same in front of the opposite sculpture. The two faces behind those had an arm protruding out of the snow. The fingers were posed so that one finger was pointing to the fifth head, which was silver bronze. The same on the opposite sculpture.

"So, boys, where's the torso?"

"Over there, detective."

Bradley walked behind the fifth head, and hanging behind it, also suspended by the piano wire, was the torso.

On the base at the front of the fifth head was the sculpture's title, *The Girl Puzzle, Nellie Bly*. Bradley quickly Googled "The Girl Puzzle" and read about the artwork which honors Nellie Bly. "By presenting, on a monumental scale, faces of many women who have endured hardship but are stronger for it. The monument gives visibility to Asian, black, young, old, immigrant, and queer women. Their stories and lives are forever commemorated alongside Nellie Bly, whose face is cast in silver bronze, while the other four faces are cast in bronze. Each of them—rendered in partial sections that appear like giant puzzle pieces—shows a depth of emotion and complexity of being broken and repaired. As the viewer approaches and enters, they become part of the puzzle by interacting with the reflective surfaces and seeing sections of the faces come together at different vantage points."

So, who the fuck is Nellie Bly? Bradley wondered and Googled.

"Elizabeth Cochrane Seaman (born Elizabeth Jane Cochran; May 5, 1864 – January 27, 1922), better known by her pen name Nellie Bly, was an American journalist who was widely known for her record-breaking trip around the world in 72 days in emulation of Jules Verne's fictional character Phileas Fogg and an exposé in which she worked undercover to report on a mental institution from within. She pioneered her field and launched a new kind of investigative journalism."

"Well, well, The Girl Puzzle," Bradley spoke quietly to herself as if realizing a deeper meaning behind this depraved killer's own art installation.

"What do we have on these security cameras, gentlemen?"

"We've asked local security to pull the footage, detective."

At that moment, one of the Island's security staff was walking over and, while overhearing the conversation started motioning his arms as if to say they had nothing.

"I'm sorry, detective. We have checked the system for the 19 camera feeds on the island, and this whole section is corrupted. The cameras are working now all over the island, but last night, from 3:00 AM to 4:00 AM, the five cameras at this end of the island show nothing but static. They must have used some sort of device

to disrupt the signal because these are all wire-
less cameras."

"What about coming on or off the island? You
must have the four access points monitored?"

"We sure do, and there was nothing and no one
that doesn't check out. Whoever did this came
by water and left by water."

Bradley suddenly looked up at the myriads of high-rise
buildings surrounding the island. She knew she was
being watched. This guy just loved to watch the murder
scene develop.

"Ok, let's get the coroner in to collect the bits
and pieces and see if they can make sense of any
of this."

Bradley noted that the limbs had been removed from
the torso in a surgical manner. Very clean and blood-
free. Like a beast hanging in a butcher shop, the torso
did not look like a murder victim but like a medical
experiment. She knew it was going to take some time to
get an ID on this body, and until then, there was nothing much left to do. The photographer was capturing
every angle and Bradley followed her around to make
sure she got every angle that might be useful and to
have another look at each body part to see if she might
be missing any clue. She was also paying particular
attention to see if there were any of those sneaky little
cameras that the killer liked to use, but she knew that
this was not the scene for that. He was up there somewhere watching.

Bradley stood for several minutes just scanning the buildings for any sign of a suspect, but also, she knew she was being observed, so it was somewhat like a conversation.

"I'm coming for you, pal," Bradley said out loud to herself with a slight snarling smile on her face. "You'll slip up. You motherfuckers always slip up."

The Bird Cage

2008. New York

Construction was progressing swiftly with Fanny Bird's capital. With all gut renovations in New York townhouses, if you can keep the outside walls and floor beams, it cuts four months off the otherwise ground-up build time. The house was magnificent. A twenty-foot wide seven-story mansion with a limestone facia, marble, and zebra wood floors, imported antique French fireplace mantles, sprawling Van Gogh granite benches, elite appliances including a sixty thousand dollar La Cornue French oven, and all showcased under resplendent coffered ceilings. People who spend over twenty million on a house expect these top-level finishes. From the spiraling sweeping hardwood staircases to the ornate gold elevator car, it was a masterpiece.

The problem, of course, was that Bradley was over budget and out of cash. The construction line was maxed out, and she still had many suppliers and contractors to pay to finish the work and get it on the market. She knew she had to refinance, and she knew that Fanny Bird would never agree to subjecting her equity to further debt even though it was Fanny encouraging the overspending and maximum opulence in the finishes.

Bradley was not foreign to "arts and crafts," as she liked to call it, meaning fudging certain documents to improve her perceived investability on paper. In this case though, she would need to forge Fanny's signature as well as her other equity partners. She called an investment bank that had bailed her out in the past, but they rejected her because she only got out of the last deal by the skin of her English teeth. Bradley was getting nervous; she had to get this house on the market. Her debt holding costs were too expensive to prolong, and if she went into default, the default rate would wipe out her equity and a sizeable percentage of the equity of her investors. Most importantly, she didn't want to lose Fanny Bird's future investment capital.

Out of the blue, her phone rang, scaring her out of her trance. She picked it up and, like an angel from heaven, she introduced herself as Brandy Find, owner of Find Capital.

> "Hey, Miss Bradley, I know you had a conversation with Charles Brevetti over at York Capital this morning, and they were not in a position to help you, but Brevetti called me because he knows we like these last-minute deals to finance the final mile on high-end projects. Last money in, first money out sort of thing. Are you still looking for a refinance?"

> "Hi Brandy, yes, I certainly am. I need to take out a five million construction loan and add one point five million in new money to finish the project."

"Ok, so six point five million at twenty percent interest and two points. Are you ok with the terms?"

"Two points is high. One hundred and thirty thousand eats into the funds I need to complete."

"Ok, so we will put the points on the loan and give you six point, six three million. With repayment due in full within six months, or you'll go to default rate. Will that work?"

"It depends on the default rate. Not that I am expecting to go over two months, let alone six months, but sometimes things don't go according to plan."

"Well, our default rate is pretty aggressive. We don't like to lose capital, so we protect ourselves. The default rate is 50% interest, but as soon as it is in default, we immediately seize the asset, wipe out the equity holders, and sell the property. Of course, we don't want that to happen, and I know you'll want to exit as early as possible. I just need to be upfront with you: If this goes into default, something has gone terribly wrong, and we act fast to secure our interests. If you can live with our terms, we will get you funded."

"Hmm. I see. Well, I can't say I have many options at this late hour, so I guess I'll have to go with it. How soon can you get me paperwork?"

"I'll get it over to you first thing in the morning, but you'll need to have all equity investors over ten percent to sign off on the deal, so it depends how long that will take as to how fast we can fund and close."

"That's fine," Bradley barked excitedly, knowing that she couldn't get Fanny to sign anyhow. "I'll get the docs back same day."

"That sounds good. Talk to you tomorrow."

Bradley slept peacefully for the first time in months, knowing that she could now get out of this deal and onto scaling her operation with Fanny Bird's capital. She woke up fresh and fired up. She already had a text from Find Capital saying the courier was already on the way with the loan documents.

The courier arrived within minutes, and Bradley sat down with her coffee to review them. She had the Fanny Bird documents on hand with Fanny's signature, and she had been practicing. If she put it behind the signing page, she could trace over it, but it had to be at a pace, or you could see interruptions in the flow. Her other investors were less than 10%, so she didn't have to forge their names. Only Fanny's.

She had that tingling sensation that she got when doing something that was a little underhand and sneaky. She'd always gotten away with her little arts and crafts ventures, so she was not worried. Nothing goes wrong when nothing goes wrong. It's only if it ends up in litigation that these things ever get discovered.

The loan closing happened swiftly. Far more swiftly than past closings. Bradley was in the clear and feeling confident. She set up a call with her equity investors to assure them that all was in order and the house would be on the market within weeks. Fanny Bird was on the call and was her usual pessimistic self, ending the call with, "We'll see dear, good luck."

It took eight weeks to get the construction completed and the certificate of occupancy issued. It was finally ready to list. Bradley had her own brokerage license so that she didn't have to pay three percent to a seller's broker, and she always negotiated with the seller's broker because the sales price was so high there was plenty of room for negotiation on the percentage. She listed on the MLS and was already fielding calls when the doorbell rang at the property. Bradley opened the door to a process server. Her heart sank. What could this possibly be? Everyone was paid, everything was done. Every box was ticked, every "i" dotted and t crossed.

Bradley ripped open the envelope, and her heart sank further with every line she read. She was being sued by the neighboring property, claiming that cracks had appeared in their walls from the construction. They were taking her to court for reparations. Bradley knew exactly what that meant. The house could not be sold while litigation was in process. The court date was set, and it was 6 weeks out. This was a disaster. She was being ordered not to sell the property until the matter was heard by the judge.

Bradley was terrified. Of all the things that could go wrong. The clock was ticking on her debt, and if it went to six months, she'd lose everything. But the next phone call was the one that would truly terrify her.

Bradley sat at the kitchen bench of her twenty-two-million-dollar mansion that was now suddenly perilously at risk which put her entire career and life at risk. She had to settle this lawsuit as soon as possible and get this house sold, so she could get clear of this sudden, debilitating nightmare.

Then the phone rang. Bradley froze when she saw the name. Fanny Bird!

"Hello, Fanny. This is an unexpected surprise."

"Yes, well, imagine my surprise being served papers on my fucking doorstep just now."

Bradley was in shock, suddenly realizing that she was so fixated on the details of the court paperwork that she had failed to notice the other parties listed in the suit. *Of course, she would be listed; she's a partner in the company* Bradley thought while belting the side of her own head with her hand.

"Oh, I'm so sorry, Fanny, yes, it's the neighboring building, and I'll deal with it instantly and have it deposed of."

"Yes, I'm sure, but that's not why I'm fucking calling, my dear."

"Oh. Really? How else can I be of service."

"Who on God's fucking spinning-ball-in-the-sky is Find Capital, why do we owe them seven million fucking dollars, how did you dispose of our original debt lender without my signature, and what the holy fucking bat mobile is going on over there?"

"Oh. I must say I am surprised you discovered all this from one court document in ten minutes."

"Yes, well, I called up miss Brandy Find as soon as I saw the document, and incidentally, I have her on the phone on conference. Miss Find, are you with us?"

"Yes, I'm here. Ms. Bird. Miss Bradley, I am shocked to find that Ms. Bird did not sign the loan documents, which means somebody else did, which puts your loan into immediate default. I'll be executing my documented and agreed right to seize the property, and I'll also be bringing in the authorities to deal with what is evidently mortgage fraud."

The phone went dead.

"Fanny, are you there?"

"It would appear you have fucked us both and lost us my capital plus ten million in profits, dear. I'll survive this. I can only imagine that you won't. Find a new career, dear. You're really fucking bad at this."

The line went dead, and Bradley slumped down onto a chaise lounge face-first.

Murder Six

Whitney Ricks was in the basement taking inventory. Tonight was going to be intense at the Troubadour in West Hollywood. The Eagle's release of their new album, The Long Run, was tonight, and a song about The Troubadour was on the album. Five hundred people were expected, and Whitney was feeling less than prepared.

Whitney had moved to Hollywood a year earlier from Yuba City after failing as a PE teacher. More specifically, she was fired for having an "inappropriate relationship" with one of her students and could no longer walk around town without people avoiding her or talking about her behind her back wherever she went.

Ready or not, it was almost showtime. Whitney was on edge for a few reasons, but the main one was her excitement to see a man who had been romancing her for a few weeks. He was a customer at the bar who Whitney found very attractive and mysterious. Nobody like that had ever been interested in her. Even though she was slender and beautiful, the local Yuba City gentlemen were not all that sophisticated, so the people who did show interest repulsed her. This guy had wandered in one evening a month earlier. He wasn't paying any attention to the live bands; he would just sit at the bar and rarely look at the stage. Eventually, Whitney noticed his disinterest in music and made note of it.

"Hey man, I've seen you in here a lot but you're never watching the bands. Why come here if not for the bands."

"People who watch music are missing the whole point. You hear all the missing elements that you don't notice because of the distraction of watching people performing. I like to hear it all; plus, I can then pay attention to other things."

"Like what?"

"Like you, for instance."

Whitney smiled sarcastically to deflect his advance and turned on her heel to serve other customers. She took an order and looked back over to see him staring straight ahead and smiling because he could see her looking at him out of the corner of his eye, like he'd anticipated the look. Over the coming weeks, he would frequent more regularly and eventually introduced himself.

"Hey, do you think our relationship has progressed enough to share names?"

"You don't know my name? Locals have been calling out my name ever since you've been coming in here."

"Well, I'm not sure I can trust them. I'd like to hear it from you," he said with a mysterious look."

"Oh, I see. Well, everyone knows me here as Tracy because that's my first name, and it was on my resume, so the staff and management called me Tracy, and I just let it go. The name I actually go by is Whitney."

"Aha. See, I told you these people couldn't be trusted. I knew it wasn't Tracy. You're not a Tracy. You're a Whitney."

"Well, look at you go Mr. perceptive. And you, you look like a… hmmm, Jonathan."

"Wow. It is Jonathan."

"Really?"

"No. I was just going with it because I didn't want to let you down. My name is Ray. Ray Fidel."

"Fidel? That's an unusual name."

"Yes, it's from the Latin fidelis, meaning faithful. Which is also unusual."

"Hmmm. Ok, Mr. Faithful. I'll just call you Ray."

"A pleasure to meet you, Ms. Whitney Ricks."

"Hey, I never told you my surname."

"No, I asked your manager. He didn't know your name was Whitney, but he was right about the Ricks."

"Hmmm, aren't you the mysterious one?"

"Oh, you have no idea."

He flashed a sinister smile and walked off, and that was the last that Whitney had seen of him. Tonight, however, she noticed his name on the guest list, and she was shyly excited. He was obviously interested in her, but he had not been back for a week. "Maybe he was playing it cool and letting me steep in my anxiety," she thought to herself.

The Eagles took the stage in a blaze of light and explosion of sound. The crowd went crazy, and the whole room was electric. Whitney was behind the bar and serving drinks in a fury, so she didn't have time to be keeping an eye out for her new suitor, but every now and then, her eyes would shoot around the room in between drink orders.

The band played for two full hours, and the club was rocking, but there was no Ray Fidel; then, during the last song, she spotted somebody way up the front wearing a cap, but that couldn't be Ray as he never even looks at the bands playing. He turned around as the band finished the song, and the club music came on. It was him alright, and Whitney stared at him, waiting for him to acknowledge her. He was walking straight towards her when suddenly he turned left and headed out the door, turning around only at the very last second to look right at her. His smile struck Whitney like ice. A chilling, cruel smile. She didn't let it affect her as she still had a lot to do before the end of the night. The club would be open until 11, so she wouldn't be home until almost midnight.

Cleanup went slow, and Whitney was exhausted. Ray's peculiar exit and eerie smile were playing on her mind more and more. She finally locked the doors with the last of the staff and headed to the parking lot, where her moped was chained up. Her house was up through Beachwood Canyon, which at this time of night was only 30 minutes on her machine. She enjoyed the ride home with the hot summer wind in her face. She always found her bike relaxing, especially after a long shift at the club. Not so nice in the rain, but on nights like these it was a joy. She hardly hit a light and was home in 25 minutes. Pulling into her drive, the image of Ray had left her mind completely and she was feeling great.

Whitney loved living on her own. Several relationships down, she was very hesitant to consider ever living with anyone again and the house she had found in the hills was pure bliss. She had rented it from a retired couple who wanted to travel overseas for an extended time and gave it to her at a rate that was almost house-sitting. All she had to do was look after Bones, the couple's old grey cat. Bones was not at all high maintenance. He would hunt creatures and feed himself so often that sometimes he wouldn't eat food in his bowl for a whole week, and she would have to throw it out. Either that or the neighbors were feeding him. Either way, he wasn't around very much, and that was just fine with Whitney.

A chilled glass of white wine later, she lit up a joint and smoked it down while she danced in front of a mirror in her almost transparent La Perla lace kimono. She imagined herself as an exotic dancer and fantasized about dancing in public—not that she would ever actually do it, but she found the idea intensely exciting. Some nights, she would dance for hours, listening to music and smoking weed.

Any thought of the club was erased from her mind, and she was now on Whitney time and might as well have been on a beach in Los Carbos. In an instant, her attention was snapped back to reality when she thought she saw something moving outside. She went to the window to look but soon realized how high it was and assumed it was an owl or something big in the flying department.

Her pulse still racing, she poured herself another prosecco and set about stilling her mind and returning to her dream state.

A knock at the door. She snapped her gaze to the clock. 1:00 AM.

"What the fuck! Who the fuck."

She looked out the peephole. Nothing. She opened the door frantically, looking around. Her heart was racing madly now, and she was in a desperate panic. Closing the door, she ran to the kitchen to find a weapon, and walking past the door to the basement she froze in her tracks when she heard a second terrifying knock. This one slower and more deliberate. Her head slowly turned to the basement door as the knob began turning. The door swung out as if by itself and emerging from the darkness of the basement steps was that cold face with that chilling smile. Without saying a word, he grabbed her neck with his left hand, and for a fleeting second, Whitney thought he was going to kiss her until his right hand gently but deliberately slid the needle into her neck. In seconds, she had lost consciousness and was draped in his arms.

He picked her up and took her over to the bedroom where she had been dancing in the mirror. Laying her gently on the ground and arranging her in a pose that he found alluring.

In the corner of his eye, he noticed movement outside. Without registering his awareness, he walked slowly to the front room, where the light was off, and he could analyze the movement outside. Sure enough, hanging in a large tree suspended by a climbing harness was a man.

Reynaldo sat frozen in place, hardly breathing. He knew it was time to get out of there, but he couldn't risk being detected. After several minutes of no activity, he decided to take a chance and slowly shimmy down the tree. Finally, Reynaldo reached the bottom of the tree and made his way back to his truck—frequently snapping back to make sure he was not being followed—and took off gingerly down the hill, being careful not to look in the direction of the house or acknowledge the emerging, menacing figure. Reynaldo's heart was beating. His mind was racing, not registering what he thought he had seen. This gut-wrenching episode had cured him of his voyeuristic addiction. It had shaken him deeply. All he wanted to do was to get back to his apartment and put this behind him forever.

The drive seemed to wind on like an endless loop, and by the time Reynaldo pulled into his driveway in East LA, he didn't even remember driving home. It was a hazy blur, and now that the shock and adrenalin was wearing off, he was exhausted. He sat in his truck with his eyes closed for ten minutes, thanking God that he had miraculously escaped detection. Eventually, he cracked the door handle and stepped out of the truck. Turning to close the truck door, he didn't have the slightest sense of the approaching figure. The ice pick slid into his back next to his left shoulder blade and pierced his heart from the back. It was such an efficient method of execution that the victim doesn't even know it has happened, they simply drop, and they're gone.

A New Day

It was several hours before Whitney Ricks became aware of her surroundings again. Opening her eyes was like looking at bright light through cotton wool. She was completely at peace and was entirely unaware of how close she had come to her last breath.

Very slowly, her memory of the evening's events started coming back to her, and she felt a creeping terror starting to wash over her. Was her attacker still in the house? What am I wearing? Am I hurt? Gently and carefully, she pulled herself upright, clutching the arm of the sofa. She looked in the mirror and realized she was mostly naked and still wearing her lace lingerie. Checking her body for any sign of violation, she suddenly remembered that her attacker could still be in the house.

Stumbling to the kitchen, she drew a large carving knife and gingerly crept room to room, eventually stopping at the basement door. Unable to turn the knob from fear of what might be waiting on the other side, she reached down and turned the key to lock it. After thoroughly checking the house and starting to feel that she might be alone again, she summoned the gumption to call 911.

Detective Sweet and her partner arrived within fifteen minutes and pulled up at the same time as the ambulance. Neighbors came out to see what was going on and Whitney went out in her sweats to show them she was okay. Detective Sweet drew her weapon, not knowing who Whitney was, but was soon put at ease when she identified herself.

> "Let's go inside, Miss Ricks; you look a little unsteady on your feet. Is there anyone still in the house?"

> "No, the house is clear; I checked everywhere. I think he's long gone."

They went inside, and Detective Sweet and her partner swept the house to make sure they were alone.

> "Do you know who it was that attacked you?"

> "Yes, it was a man from the club where I work. He's been coming around for the past few months, and last night, I saw him again at the end of the night, but he disappeared. I was home for a few hours when I heard a knock at the basement door."

> "The basement door?"

> "Yes, I thought it was the front door at first, but after checking, I realized the knock was coming from the basement. As soon as I opened the door, he lurched forward and stabbed me in the neck with something, and I was out. He laid me on the floor over there."

"How do you know where he laid you if you were unconscious?"

"Well, for one, I woke up there, but actually, I had this awareness of where I was. Sort of like being under an anesthetic, but you know the surgeon is there, which happened to me once. This was very similar. And I remember him being very gentle with me. Maybe it was just whatever he drugged me with, but I was very calm and at peace even though I was basically naked, and he had attacked me. He seemed to be posing me with great care, but then he just left."

"Hmm. That seems a little strange to go to all that trouble and then just leave. Maybe he was disturbed."

Detective Sweet looked out the window which was the only direct line to be able to see anything outside the house.

"Hey, Vinnie," she yelled for her partner. "Can you meander down there at the base of that large tree and see if there is any sign of disturbance?"

"Will do," said happy go lucky Vinnie.

Minutes later, Vinnie was yelling from outside.

"Yo, Sweet. I found something here."

Walking enthusiastically over to the window, Sweet looks down to see Vinnie standing at the large tree.

"What you got, Vinnie?"

"Someone was here for sure. There are fresh footsteps and there's bark off around the tree where he put the climbing lanyard, and fresh spur holes where he climbed up very recently."

"Thanks, Vinnie, good work. So, Miss Ricks, your assailant was almost definitely disturbed by somebody, and that is probably the reason you are still alive."

Detective Sweet saw the look of horror come over Whitney Ricks' face.

"If I were you, I'd be finding somewhere else to stay right now,"

"Oh, don't worry, detective, as soon as you leave, I'm out of here."

"Ok, but you need to be examined by the medics for our report, and I need details of where you will be if we need to reach out again."

"No problem, I'll be at my parents' place in Yuba City until I can get myself together to do what's next. Whatever it is, it won't be in Hollywood."

The medics came in and examined Whitney while Detective Sweet continued with her questioning. Eventually, everyone left, and Whitney got to work packing her belongings into her suitcase to make the 400-mile trip home to Yuba City. She couldn't carry her gear on the moped, so she'd have to rent a car. Riding her moped down to the West Hollywood Avis car rental office, Whitney played the surreal events of last evening over and over in her mind. Struggling to comprehend how imminent her demise may have been, she decided to use it as a second chance lease on life, and she was, surprisingly, beginning to get inspired.

The Avis crew helped load her moped into the trunk of the Buick Electra, and she drove back up to the house to pick up her bags. On the way out of town, she stopped in at the Troubadour to tell them she was leaving town for good and to watch out for Ray Fidel or whatever his name was, but the manager and staff had already had a visit from Detective Sweet.

The staff all wished Whitney well as she wandered out the door of the Troubadour for the last time. As she stood in the parking lot about to get in her rented Buick, she slowly looked around, suddenly feeling an eerie sensation of being watched, but soon realized that considering what she had been through, it would be some time before she started to feel normal again. She got in the car, lit up a joint, blasted a tune on the radio, and took off up Sunset at sunset.

* * *

Living back home with her parents was a step backward, but Whitney didn't mind. She was taking time to get her head right. After eight weeks, she was getting itchy feet and had been investigating possibilities. Possible places to live, possible careers to begin, and possible futures to imagine. It had taken time for her change of name to become official, but two months after the most terrifying incident of her life, Whitney Ricks was leaving for New York City for an interview with a diamond dealership on West 47th St under her new name, Alexis Anna Riccardi.

Murder Seven

Bradley woke up with a strange and foreign eupho-ria. It was Saturday morning, and she had abso-lutely nothing to do. It was not immediately apparent why she felt so clear and uplifted, but as she thought it through, she wondered if it were possible that she was getting closer to capturing this elusive madman. Her perspective had changed. She was switching from the back foot to the front and starting to somehow under-stand the mind of this asshole that was taunting her.

The most recent murder scene was something dif-ferent, something sick. Like it had lost its normal sense of humor and become something darker and even more macabre. This could mean that she was closing in on him, and he was starting to show signs of desperation or at least becoming more extreme, which meant more likely to make a mistake. Was he trying to impress her?

She poured herself a hot cup of tea and wandered out onto her terrace overlooking the Hudson River. Standing out there in a peaceful and fully absorbed trance with her elbows leaning on the terrace rail and her cup of tea held with both hands, she was snapped back to the present by the intense and demanding sound of her cell phone ring-ing. Glancing at the screen, she held the phone to her ear.

"Captain M. What a delightful surprise on a sunny Saturday morning."

"Bradley, are you mocking me?"

"Mocking you? Captain, I'm having a rare and bewilderingly enjoyable day for the first time in years. I'm not even hung over. I'm simply sharing my joy with you."

"Hmm. Is that so? Well, it's about to get worse."

"Well, you do have a way."

"Shut up, Bradley."

"Yes, of course, Sir."

"How do you feel about London?"

"Aside from being born there and regretting the day I ever left to come to this crazy circus freak show?"

"Well, alright. Your ticket is waiting at JFK. Your guy is upsetting the shit out of the English. Which I'm fucking thrilled about because he's not here upsetting the shit out of me, and I get to have some peace for a minute because you'll be the hell outta my fucking hair. Let me know what you find out, and don't rush back."

"Will do, Capt. And tha…"

He'd already hung up. Bradley showered, packed, and got in her silver Range Rover to head to the airport. Everything was going so smoothly that she just didn't trust it. No traffic, no assholes, no phone calls. Just then, the phone rang.

"Detective Bradley, it's Chief Inspector Willoughby from Homicide and Major Crime Command in London."

"Chief Inspector. Thank you for reaching out. Captain Merrick hasn't told me anything yet. I'm about to hop on a plane to you but what can you share before I arrive? Specifically, why do you think it's the guy I'm tracking?"

"Yes, well, I'm not sure who we're dealing with, but your name and division were written on the hind quarters."

"The hind quarters of what?"

"The horse."

"The Horse?"

"Look, I'm being called into a meeting; I'll brief you at Heathrow when you land. Talk soon."

"A fucking horse?" Bradley said to herself.

Bradley got to JFK at her usual blinding and mostly illegal pace, parked in long term, and trotted off to the British Airways Terminal 8, where her ticket was indeed waiting for her.

She was strangely excited about going back to the mother country. Surprising to herself was the fact that she may have been missing her parents. The idea of seeing her old haunts and friends was heightening an already enchanting Saturday.

Seven stiff bourbons on the plane and her mind was racing as she focused and reflected more and more on the strangely artistic, albeit lurid killings. She scanned the news for any horse-related London murders but realized it must have been too early for the press to get hold of it.

Awakening from her boozy afternoon haze as the wheels met the world again, Bradley took a second to recalibrate where she was and why she was there. Deplaning was faster than normal as she was prioritized by the cabin crew, who had obviously been alerted. Bradley was liking the special treatment very much. She could certainly get used to this. As soon as she cleared the jetway, she was approached by an obsessively English-looking chap who she quickly deduced was Chief Inspector Willoughby.

"Detective Bradley?"

"Chief Inspector, nice to meet you." Shaking his hand with exuberant might.

"Call me Willy."

"Your name is Willy Willoughby?"

"Yes. Well, William, but everybody calls me Willy."

"Well then. Call me Bradley."

"You don't have a first name?"

"Not really, no, I'm more of the Madonna, Cher type detective."

"Yes… quite. So, here's the thing, Bradley," chimed Willoughby, having spent quite enough time on pleasantries with somebody that clearly didn't warm to them. "This is all very hush-hush as the royals are involved. The incident took place at the Palace, unfortunately and although it was not one of the royal horses in question, the Palace is most distressed at the sort of attention this will bring. The fact that a dead person gained access to the Palace has alarmed the powers that be to an extraordinary level."

"Ok, you realize, Willo, that I have no fucking clue what the fuckety-fuck you're on about. Can you take me back to the top of the page and start again do you think?"

"Willy or Willoughby will do," Bradley rolled her eyes, realizing she was in the hands of a toffy snot goblin. "At 10:00 PM last evening, two mounted police officers were taking their scheduled beat. On certain occasions, the police horses are stabled at the Royal Mews and with a special event occurring this week at the Palace, several mounted details were provisioned. While making their rounds, they were returning over Westminster Bridge, past Big Ben, and came upon the statue of Churchill, where they saw two young urchins defacing Sir Winston's memorial with paint and props. The two juveniles, of course, fled in two different directions as the officers approached, at which point the officers split up and gave chase.

It would appear that the stunt was a decoy designed to separate the officers and isolate a target. One officer dismounted and chased the assailant into the tube and down one of the track tunnels toward Picadilly Circus. This left the other officer to follow his target into a private gated garden two suburbs away.

Within seconds of entering the gate of the private garden, the officer was pulled from his horse and sedated."

"It was the officer that was killed?"

"No. Do pay attention, as we're just getting started.

"What a tosspot," Bradley thought to herself while CI Dickhead waffled his way along.

"You see, Bradley, the officer was accosted, pulled from his steed, laid to the ground, and sedated. The unconscious officer was then placed back on his animal, strapped into the saddle, and a contraption was added to keep him upright. Sort of a metal L-shaped device on which the officer sat while being tethered to the upright post. Then—would you believe—an already deceased female was strapped to his back, naked, don't you know. The whole thing is quite lewd and disgraceful.

It was raining last evening, so the rain accoutréments concealed the dead woman tethered behind the officer. Now, the thing is, Bradley, these animals are so well trained that they don't need direction; a slap on the rump, and they're off home."

"Yes, that's how I do it."

"What?"

"Nothing, carry on."

"So the horse, not having any direction from its rider, simply trudged on back through the rain to the Royal Mews. On arrival, the guard opened the gate to receive the officer and his horse as usual. Of course, once inside the Palace walls, the guard enquired as to the whereabouts of his beat partner and received no response. It was then that the naked truth was revealed, quite literally, I'm afraid. The victim was untethered and brought down for examination, at which point it was discovered that the poor girl had been bayoneted with an ice pick through the back just off the left shoulder blade directly into her heart. Her body had been painted with an elaborate map, like a full body tattoo. The map outlined all the murders that this perpetrator had apparently committed, all of which evidently connected to you as your name and branch were emblazoned in the same red ink on the horse's ass. No malice intended."

"Oh, of course not. So, when do I get to see this naked work of art?"

"Well, we are arriving now."

Willoughby pulled the car into the gate of the Royal Mews, and the gate promptly opened. They drove on through into the courtyard and alighted the vehicle. The Crown Equerry—the operational head—and the Master of the Horse, the titular head of the Royal Mews, were there to welcome the pair. Pleasantries exchanged, the Master of the Horse, Baron Ashton, led Bradley and Willoughby through to the inner sanctum of the Mews—the heart of the Palace grounds.

Bradley could not help but be overwhelmingly enamored with her predicament. What stories she would have for her dear mother when she finally got to see her. What glee would she bathe in when presenting her adventures to the person who always seemed disappointed with her daughter's lack of ascension to any worthy—in her lofty opinion—vocation?

They entered a tack room just off the stables, and laying there on a workbench was the victim. Willoughby pulled back the horse blanket that covered her, and there she lay in naked grandeur, covered head to toe in red illustration. Bradley was visibly shaken.

"Detective Bradley? Are you alright? Surely, you've seen a naked victim before?"

"Not only have I seen a naked victim before, Chief Inspector, but I've seen this naked victim before. This is Jenny Scattergood. I went to school with her. I worked with her in banking."

"She was a friend?"

"No, not at all. I hated her. She made my life miserable. She was a bully, a gossip, and a manipulative cow. But I certainly wouldn't have wished her dead. I haven't even thought about her in decades. Except for…"

"Except for what, Bradley?"

"Oh, it's just that the last time I even mentioned her name was with somebody I met in Mexico at Puerto Vallarta 10 years ago. I was sharing some of the misery of my childhood with some guy I had met at the bar. I can't even remember his name now. Oh, I think his name was Bradley. Yes, because we laughed about having the same name. Bradley Finny."

"Ok, we will check that out. The photographer is coming in to capture the images on the body, so we can study them in detail."

Bradley had already begun examining her arch nemesis. On the bottom of her foot was the words Alexis Apthorp, the first name and location of the first victim. The road map followed her leg to the back of the knee, where the words Audrey Park were inscribed. The road continued up the inner thigh and around to the victim's hip, where it read Talia Riverside.

Bradley wondered why Alexai Freeman was not mentioned as he was murdered with Talia Nistratov. That was indeed perplexing. The map continued across the navel and around the back of the victim. Bradley lifted Jenny Scattergood's body onto its side, and right in the middle of her back were the words, Kelly Roosevelt. *Now that's interesting*, thought Bradley. *We have not identified who the Roosevelt Island victim was.*

On a curious whim, Bradley had an idea. She opened her personal email and searched for Kelly Roosevelt. There she was. A real estate broker who had been involved in a deal years earlier in which Bradley had lost a lot of money due to the broker not disclosing a pending lawsuit that would hold up construction for two years. It nearly bankrupted her. Bradley had never met the broker personally, only over the phone.

Bradley called Merrick and asked him to check on the whereabouts of a Kelly Roosevelt, real estate broker in Manhattan. Sure enough, a quick search revealed that Kelly Roosevelt was a missing person. This was the second victim that was connected to Bradley directly, and it was becoming clear to her that this had gotten intensely personal and exponentially more terrifying. Not wanting to complicate the situation and raise any suspicion unnecessarily, Bradley kept quiet to Willoughby about what was unfolding and continued analyzing the body. The map led around to the victim's right shoulder, where it read Jenny Buckingham. Considering that brought the murders up to date, Bradley was intrigued about where the map would lead next. It led down under the victim's right breast and up through her cleavage. Then, across to her left inner arm and down to the inner forearm where the words Reynaldo El Sorano were inscribed.

"Hmm. El Sorano. From the pattern, this is obviously a place," Bradley said out loud to herself.

"What's that, Bradley?"

"Oh, nothing, Chief, just thinking out loud."

Bradley pulled out her phone and typed in El Sorano. The top hit was a suburb of Eastside Los Angeles. Calling Captain Merrick again would not be well received so she made a note to investigate further. A murder in East LA with the first name Reynaldo was surely to produce a lot of results.

Bradley continued following the map.

"Are you almost done here, Detective?" griped Willoughby while pacing back and forth. "The coroner would like to take over and the Palace staff are getting a little antsy. They'd very much like to have one less dead body on the grounds."

"Yes, just about done here. A few more stops to make on this rather unpleasant journey."

From the inner forearm, the path led up the back of the arm and behind the victim's neck. Turning the victim back on her side and lifting her hair, she read the words that hit her like an electric shock. Bradley, Monaco? Was this an invitation? Was this a threat?

"Detective Bradley. What is it? You've gone a little peaked. Are you alright?"

"Yes, just found my name on the victim. Probably a coincidence. I'm sure he is not planning to murder me. But if he is, it'll be in Monaco, evidently."

"I see; well, this will all be photographed, and I'll make sure you have access to all the materials. Can we hand it over to the coroner now?"

"Yes, why not. But can we question the officer who was riding the horse?"

"We could, but all he knows is riding into the private garden and then waking up here in rather a state an hour after he rode in. He didn't see his attacker, so he won't be much use, I'm afraid."

"I understand, but I'd still like to talk to him."

"Very good, right this way."

They walked back through the stables and into a lounge where the two officers were sitting together.

"Gentlemen, this is Detective Bradley from Homicide in New York. She'd like to ask you a few questions if you don't mind."

"Certainly, but I don't know how much use we will be. Eric was chasing the other bloke, and I didn't see a thing after following my assailant into the private garden."

"Yes, I appreciate that, but did you hear anything, smell anything, or perceive anything that might give us any insight?"

"No, all I heard was a man's voice saying, 'Welcome, Officer Dinkley,' and then I was pulled from my horse and felt a sharp stabbing in my neck. I thought I was done for. I was very surprised waking up at the Mews. I had no idea how I got back here."

"So, he knew you?"

"What's that?"

"You said he called you by name. Officer Dinkley."

"Oh. Yes. I suppose he did. I'm sorry. I'm still a little foggy. Whatever he drugged me with was powerful stuff. I only woke up a few hours ago."

"So, if the Churchill vandals were a planned diversion, how do you think he knew which one of you would end up in the garden?"

"I've no idea, Detective. Maybe he researched who we both are."

"Ok, thank you both for your help. Please let Chief Inspector Willoughby know if you think of anything else and he'll be in touch with me. Ok, Chief Inspector, if you'd be so kind as to drop me back at Heathrow, I'll be off to Monaco."

"It's getting a little late for a flight to Nice tonight, Detective. Why don't you stay in London overnight and fly tomorrow."

"Yes, yes, I think I'll do that. Anywhere you can suggest for a hotel."

"One of my favorites is the Leonardo down by the tower bridge."

"Great, I'll head there. Thank you, Chief Inspector, for all your help."

"You're welcome, Detective. But I'll drive you over to the hotel if you like."

"Thank you very much. I'd appreciate it."

Bradley had warmed to Willy Willoughby. Or maybe she was feeling vulnerable. She had certainly lost her enthusiasm to see her parents after seeing the last inscription on Jenny Scattergood's body. With the close personal nature of the serial killer's attention, she didn't want to involve her family in any way. Bradley, Monaco? It certainly sounded like an invitation. Perhaps a saving grace was that all the other names on the Scattergood schematic were first-name+location. It wasn't Madeline Monaco. That made her feel a little better. But why Bradley?

After Willoughby dropped her at the Leonardo Royal, Bradley checked into her room and promptly took herself out for a walk down by the London Tower Bridge. It was a chilly evening, and looked like it may snow. The water was choppy and matched her dark, fragile mood. She played the events of the day over and over in her mind. The graphic image of Jenny Scattergood's naked body covered in red drawings. The discovery that she knew the Roosevelt Island victim.

What connection did these other murders have to her? Or were they just pawns in a strange game of Catch Me if You Can? Somehow, Bradley Finny was connected here. That strange, alluring man she had met a decade ago and with whom she had spent such a close and engaging evening. *He thought I'd make a great detective. I told him about Jenny Scattergood, and, come to think of it, I told him about Kelly Roosevelt and the harm she had caused me. What else did I tell him? And is this my serial killer? I can't imagine it. That soulful, artistic, warm, and witty man. I just can't imagine it.* Bradley's internal questions had gotten too much. She turned to walk back to the hotel and stopped in her tracks. She looked downriver back to the Tower Bridge from the dock where she had been standing. A figure stood on the bridge watching her. She stopped and stared at the figure for almost a minute. Frozen to the spot, she felt that feeling she had felt in New York. Being watched. In the presence of something unnatural. Another figure approached; it was a woman. They embraced and kissed. Bradley—suddenly realizing that the figure was just a random tourist out with his wife and not a crazed serial killer—checked herself and assumed that she was going a bit nutty after the events of the day.

Making her way back to the Leonardo, snow started to fall. The path turned wistfully quiet as she was transported back to her youth on London's historic streets. Finally unlocking her hotel room door, she looked around the room, checking that she was alone. Again, she checked herself, knowing that she was now totally paranoid. As she went to pull back the covers, she noticed chocolates on her pillow. But not just any ordinary chocolate; these had initials on them. MB in fancy writing. Quite a nice, personalized touch, she thought, pulling back the covers and hopping into the warm, soft, and inviting bed.

Murder Chess

Pulling back the drapes to reveal a snow-covered London, Bradley was thrilled to realize it was Sunday morning. She went downstairs, where a gigantic swimming pool, sauna, and steam room welcomed her. *A Sunday morning off.* I think so, she thought to herself peacefully. As she steamed, she plotted her day. Gatwick airport, a flight to Nice, and a cab to Monte Carlo. She had once stayed down on the water at the Monte Carlo Bay Resort, way back in her real estate development, money-hunting party days. Once out of the steam, she pulled out her computer and got to work booking her travel and accommodation. Having no idea what she would do when she got to Monte Carlo, she just assumed she'd be somehow notified of a next move. Perhaps another murder.

Once her flight and hotel were booked, she showered in the locker room, went upstairs, and packed. Checking out, she thanked the attendee at the desk for the thoughtful, personalized chocolates.

"Chocolates, Madam?"

"Yes, I loved the chocolates on my pillow with my initials on top."

"Umm, I don't think so. We used to place chocolates, but not for the past year or two. In fact, I think we stopped that practice during the pandemic and never started it up again."

Bradley stared blankly at the clerk. She looked back toward the elevator and back out to the front door of the hotel, trying to calculate how somebody might have gained access to her room.

"Did anyone come asking after me last evening while I was out?"

"Ah, yes, I believe somebody was enquiring after you. Another guest, in fact."

"Do you have him on security camera?"

"Well, yes, madam, but I am not authorized to…"

Bradley whipped out her badge and introduced herself.

"Detective Bradley, Homicide. I'm on official police business, and I need to see that footage now."

"Isn't that an American police badge, Miss Bradley?"

"That's right fucking now, you precious little mother fucker. This is life and death."

"Yes, Ma'am."

"And fuck you with the Ma'am, I'm just going to say. Do I look like I have a stable of hookers under my care?"

The clerk gingerly led Bradley to the back office to review the footage. He quickly pulled up the computer program and entered the approximate time frame of the desk visit. Scrubbing through and jumping to motion events, they quickly arrived at the moment. Bradley froze. It was him—from a decade ago in Mexico.

"That guy! He's a guest here?"

"Yes, Inspector."

"Detective."

"Yes, Detective Bradley. He checked out just an hour ago."

"What is that man's name?"

"Ah, let me check," taking over the computer and switching to the lodging software. "I think his name was Finny. Yes, here it is. Mr. Bradley Finny."

Bradley leapt up and exited the room without saying a word, then stormed back in.

"Send me that footage to the email on this card."

"Yes, Ma..." a murderous look from Bradley, "Yes, Detective Bradley."

Bradley got straight in a cab that was waiting outside the hotel and headed to Gatwick Airport. On the way, she called Captain Merrick, who was still sleeping, on his cell.

"Bradley, do you even care what time it is?"

"Yes, 10:30 AM, Captain now here's what's going on. The murderer's name or possibly an alias is Brad Finny."

"Bradley, it is 4:30 in the morning; what do you want me to do with this at 4:30 in the morning?"

"Oh. Yes. Well, sorry. As you were. Just sharing as we collect facts here. Talk more tomorrow. I'm off to Monaco." She hung up the phone.

"Monaco? Bradley? Bradley! This woman will be the death of me. What the hell is she doing in Monaco? I'm going back to damn sleep."

Bradley's head was spinning. These names were all coming together. Bradley Finny. *Wait,* Bradley thought to herself. She started to write down all the names from her past with an F or a B. "Fanny Bird, Oh my god no." The cab driver looked at her, but she waved him off. *Brandy Find, Find capital. Smart ass. He's been at this the whole time. Darby Finn, the alias he used for Dr. Mayor.* It was all coming together and making sense now. An elaborate web was beginning to unfold in some sort of masterminded decade-long game of murder chess. *Fanny Bird? Could he have played her to play me? I never saw her in person, only on those dark, blurry video calls.*

That would mean he bankrupted me, forced me out of real estate, and had me indicted. Her wild ride of thought revelation continued through airport security and onto the plane to Nice. She replayed every moment she could remember of their conversations in Puerta Vallarta. *He told me I'd make a great detective. Did he somehow manipulate me into becoming a fucking detective? This is insane. Who is this lunatic? This is a whole other level of fucked up. The mortgage broker, who the hell else did he plant into my life to derail me? He played them all.*

* * *

The plane touched down in Nice a little after 3:00 PM Sunday afternoon. It was warm and sunny, a welcome change for Bradley in the usually chilly January. She had several missed calls from Captain America, and she was, on the one hand, eager to talk to him but, on the other hand, nervous about how much to share knowing what she now knew. It seems she was far more deeply involved in these murders than she had ever imagined. This could even cast suspicion on her. She was not sure how, but she was starting to think it, and who knows how deep this went.

She flew through customs and got into a cab to take the 30-minute journey over to the Principality of Monaco. Her earlier days of high living were coming back to her in spades at this point. She remembered landing in Nice in a private jet and helicoptering over to the Bay Hotel. In what grand style she lived in those golden carefree days. When dealing in millions, the perks were everywhere; the nights were endless, and the days but a blink.

As the cab pulled into the Monte Carlo Bay Hotel, her mind was fully living the magic moments of her 20-year-ago self. The cab door opened, and she was instantly whipped back to reality. Nobody knew her name, and she was in a cab, not a limousine. Checking into her room, she asked if anyone had been asking after her.

> "No, I am afraid there are no messages for you, Mademoiselle Bradley. I hope you enjoy your stay with us."

Her room was extraordinary and just as she remembered. Overlooking the palatial grounds out to the sun-speckled Mediterranean, which drowned all misery and washed away the sins of every man and woman. She loved that ocean. It went with wine, roses, and a carefree life that she longed for so much more than she ever thought possible. These memories were doing her no good as her current predicament became more and more real, terrifying, and bizarre. *What could Bradley Finny, or whatever his fucking name is, want with me and my stupid little life?*

Either way, it was time for a very stiff drink and a cigar just inside the open doors of the generous terrace that she left a lifetime ago. Tonight, she would try to relive her carefree days and live in denial in the safe surrounds of the concrete walls of her beautiful sanctuary, if only for an evening. Cracking open the marvelous duty-free, double size bottle of some fancy bullshit bourbon she'd found at the airport, filling a glass with crystal clear ice, and pouring a generous dose of medicine, Bradley sat back in her soft leather Chesterfield chair, stretched her legs on to the mohair footstool, lit a Cohiba, and clinked her glass to her reflection's glass in the hotel mirror. The late afternoon sun gently filled the room through the terrace curtains, which breathed in and out in sync with the Mediterranean waves. At peace once more—if but for a moment.

Murder Eight

Dr. Johanna Mayor sat marking papers in her Harvard office. For some reason, she was ill at ease. Detective Bradley's visit the month prior had stirred up the past in her blood. The image of Darby Finn still haunted her. Especially now being even more certain of his intentions at the time.

It was Sunday afternoon, and Dr. Mayor liked to work in her office on quiet, sunny Sundays due to the solitude. Usually, she would be writing, but getting the paper grading out of the way cleared the decks for a nice blank canvas so she could fully focus on her writing. Writing was the pleasure—the favorite food that you leave for last on your plate to enjoy it at the end. Everything else was just in the way of the writing, so it had to be completed before her mind would not feel guilty writing when there was niggling work to be done.

Finally, she finished the last paper and gave it an A. There were still issues with the work, but she knew this student came from a difficult place and had worked harder than anyone else to get there. The effort alone warranted a full extra grade, and she knew the surprise of an A would be such an inspiration she would work even harder as a result. Some students just had that ethic, and Johanna knew how to bring out the best in them. The obnoxious assholes needed punishment, so she would down-mark them just to keep their little narcissistic inside monster in check, even if their work was up to snuff.

Through the thousands of students that had passed through her purview, she had learned that the psychology was more important than the teaching. Teaching them how to learn and how to minimize the possibility of coming a cropper was a far greater gift than any textbook knowledge she might impart. Rewarding good character was the mark of a great teacher, in Dr. Mayor's opinion. Knocking the slubberdegullion out of entitled little twats that had never been told no was just a simple pleasure of the job.

Thrilled with her afternoon's solace and deck-clearing accomplishment, Dr. Mayor packed her leather satchel—a gift from her late husband that she cherished—and strolled off across the causeway bridge back through the main campus, past Massachusetts Hall, Annenberg Hall, Harvard Hall, and across the Harvard Yard. She loved her little commute to her home on the other side of campus. All the history, all the great minds that had passed through these grounds. It was the richness of these small pleasures that made her life truly fulfilling. Running her finger across the solid gold initials on her soft leather satchel always reminded her to appreciate the small things. The memories and symbols by which one measures their grand moments. As far as she was concerned, joy could only be achieved if it could be found in the smallest of pleasures. Then the large pleasures were a gift, and the troubles could be more easily overcome.

Eventually arriving at her small cottage a few blocks off campus, she removed her shoes, unlocked the front door, and put her hand in to turn on the hall light. As she walked through the door, she was set upon by a fur-coated Persian assassin seeking food and attention.

"Hello, Ruth, my darling."

She named her cat Ruth Bader Ginsberg in honor of her fellow Harvard alumna.

"How are you, my dear? Humbly striving for democracy and justice for all, no doubt."

"Hello, Johanna."

Dr. Mayor froze in her tracks without turning her head to see what she already knew. The voice of her demise. No wonder he had been on her mind.

"Why now? After all these years, Mr. Finn?"

"Well, my affairs here are coming to a close and you are a loose end. One that may have brought me undone. That, and I like a nice, tidy story. Our adventure started so long ago, and to bookend it just puts a lovely bow on our time together."

Turning to face her assassin. "But what is it that drives you? What on earth gave you the idea to target me? I want to at least understand the thinking that is snuffing out my life."

"You were my first, Dr. I've always lived with this darkness, and it took me a long time to work out that this feeling can only be subdued by feeding it. Getting rid of temptation is simple, you see. You just give in to it, and it is gone until the next one arrives. Why fight against it? Why live every day in pain and resistance? If I were an alcoholic, I'd simply take a drink. This is far healthier, don't you think?"

"Well, no. Not for me."

Darby Finn laughed heartily. "Don't you see, Dr. This is why I fell in love with the idea of taking your life in the first place? You are truly worthy. Just imagine, if we were not interrupted the first time all those years ago, your days would have been very much shorter. It has been a pleasure, Dr."

With that, he lunged forward and, drove the hypodermic needle into her neck and closed the plunger of the syringe.

Murder Nine

At 9:00 PM Sunday evening, Bradley awoke with a heart-starting jolt, still in her chair at the Monte Carlo Bay Hotel. With the terrace doors open and the sun having set hours earlier, she was freezing cold. Shivering and rubbing her arms, she scuffled into the bathroom and ran a hot bath. Not waiting for it to fill, she jumped straight in and let the beautiful warm water run over her. She sat in the bath with her arms around her legs, shivering until she slowly warmed up and relaxed into the delightful water which had risen to her neck.

As she bathed, she started to think about food. Realizing she had not eaten since London, she decided to take herself out to dinner at the casino. She was, after all, in Monte Carlo. It did occur to her that her life may well be in danger, but who kills people at a casino on a Sunday night? That would be the height of rudeness.

Just then, her doorbell rang in her suite.

"Oh fuck. What now. Yes?" She yelled loudly with a tone that left nobody wondering if she were annoyed.

"Yes, Miss Bradley, I have a message for you."

"I'm in the bath; can you just tell me what it is?"

"No, mademoiselle, it is a handwritten, sealed envelope."

"Just slide it under the door, merci beaucoup. Au revoir."

Having exhausted her two-phrase French vocabulary she felt he should be thankful that she even gave it a go. The bellman rolled his eyes slightly and slipped the note under the door, realizing that his chance of receiving a tip was now extremely unlikely.

After 20 minutes of magnificent bathing, Bradley dragged her now hungover ass out of the tub and wrapped herself in warm towels that had been cooking on the warming rack. She then pulled on an oversized soft robe and slid her feet into the luxurious hotel slippers. Walking out to her hallway she noticed the envelope which had been slid under the door that she had already forgotten about.

Curious but apprehensive, she opened the sealed envelope and dropped down into her chair, the room now having warmed up after closing the terrace doors. She closed her eyes and braced herself. She had been waiting for something, but who knew what?

"Dear Madeline," the letter began. "Thank you so much for coming to Monaco. I realize my invitation was somewhat dramatic but now you are here, I would like to see you. Our time in Puerta Vallarta is one of my fondest memories, and I would like to revisit our time together. Fear not; you will be safe with me, and I will share everything that has happened over the last decade. I am sure you have many questions to ask. I have arranged for a special private dinner in my suite on Monday evening at 7:00 PM. Ask the hotel manager for a key to Mr. Finny's room. He is expecting you."

Yours kindly

Bradley Finny.

Why would he have me ask for a key? Why wouldn't he just answer the damn door? Stranger and stranger. But I suppose I have come this far. And I'll have a gun. So, what's the harm?

Bradley still could not imagine the man she had met in Mexico doing any of the things that she had witnessed, but she had to find out. It seemed so out of character.

Realizing she was now bordering on starvation, she got dressed and prepared to head to the Monte Carlo Casino for dinner. Surely, after going to all the trouble of setting up such an elaborate meeting, she would be safe until tomorrow night. The hotel limo was waiting out the front to shuttle people to the casino on demand. She slid into the long black Bentley and slumped back enthusiastically into the plush leather, once again remembering her old life.

Monte Carlo Casino was just as she remembered it, besides a few modernizations and upgrades. After a beautiful two Michelin Star dinner and a bottle of spectacular Californian wine—she hated French wine, fuck the pretentious froggy snob pricks and their bullshit wine, she thought to herself—she hit the casino to risk a hundred euros. Bradley was not much of a gambler but "when in Monaco," as they say. All in all, a fabulous evening, considering she was probably in town to be killed. She even picked up five hundred euros on the roulette table. The hotel Limo pulled up outside the casino at the stroke of twelve as expected and she dropped herself in the back seat with sated enthusiasm. "That'll do, Monaco," she said to herself as her chauffeur whisked her back to her palatial hotel through the storied streets of Monte Carlo.

After sleeping through the morning and a good part of the afternoon, Bradley woke up to the hotel phone ringing.

> "Bradley, what the goddamn hell are you doing? I've been trying to call you for three God damn days."

> "Captain. How nice to hear from you. Sorry, my phone has no calling plan here in France, so it has been offline, or I would have been in touch. My apologies. But how did you find me here?"

> "I've been calling hotels in Monaco for two hours. Naturally, I found you at the most opulent one. I hope you don't think you're expensing this little vacation of yours?"

> "Vacation? Captain, I am here following a very specific lead, and I do believe I may be on to the killer, and an arrest is imminent."

> "Oh, you think so, do you? Well, I hate to be the bearer of bad news and all but unfortunately,

you're dead wrong. You remember your Harvard Professor, Dr. Mayor?"

"Yes, of course."

"Well, she's dead, and it was your guy. As usual, your name is all over the damn place. So, get your ass back here because your killer ain't in Monte fucking Carlo; he's in Cambridge Massa-fucking-chusetts."

Bradley was silent for a moment and slightly in shock hearing that Dr. Mayor had been murdered. "Can you describe the scene for me, Captain?"

"Well, it's kinda bizarre, but not for you. You seem to get such a kick out of these grotesque posings. She was strapped to a large ornate chair from her own house and then placed in the Harvard Yard directly in front of the statue of John Harvard."

"Anything strange about the scene?"

"Yes, the killer removed her left shoe and sock. Something about rubbing the foot of the famous statue or something. Some sort of tribute to her tenure at Harvard and the legacy of the founder. I don't know; I have no patience for these academic mind games. Just get here and deal with it, will you!"

"I see. Ok, Captain, I'll book a flight out first thing in the morning."

"In the morning, my ass, Bradley, get to the airport right fucking now."

"Can't do it, Captain. No flights out of Nice until 9:00 AM and none direct to New York, so I'll have to go through London or Barcelona, but I will be there as soon as I can."

There was no point in explaining her evening dinner plans to Captain Merrick. She didn't know what was going on, but she had to be there at 7:00 PM tonight to try and make sense of any of it.

"Oh, and by the way, while you've been out jet-setting I've been here doing actual police work, and I followed up that lead. A man called Reynaldo Sanchez was murdered in 1979 in El Sorano, East LA. He was stabbed through the heart from the back with an ice pick. I don't know what that means to you, but that is the only thing we have on record."

"I see. That name was written on the corpse of Jenny Scattergood in London as one of the murders that were mapped out on her body."

"Well, I'd certainly know that if I ever received a report from you, Bradley. Imagine that."

"Yes, it is on its way, Captain and a fine report it will be. Must go. See you in a jiffy."

"A fucking jiffy? What the fuck is a jiffy? Bradley?"

It was only 4:00 PM, so Bradley decided a swim was in order down in the extravagant labyrinth of swimming facilities that wound their way through the lavish oceanfront Monte Carlo Bay property.

As the hours ticked by, Bradley became more and more apprehensive. What waited for her an hour from now? *Who was Bradley Finny, and what did he have in store for her? Did he murder all these people, or is there some other explanation for these bizarre and twisted events?*

She headed upstairs to her room and dressed in the most suitable thing she could find to be dined, fucked, or murdered in. She had not exactly packed eveningwear. All she had was a sheer black suit. That would have to do. She checked her gun, which was locked in her police travel case that got it through airports, and slid it into her jacket pocket. She was ready. Heading to the lobby, her senses were heightened to the point her ears were ringing. She found the hotel manager and presented herself. He was indeed expecting her and slipped his hand in his jacket pocket and pulled out a hotel key.

"Room 777, mademoiselle, Monsieur Finny welcomes your attendance."

"Yes. We shall see about that. Merci."

"De rien, mademoiselle."

Bradley stepped into the elevator and pressed seven. The floors pinged by with agonizing lethargy. Finally, the doors opened on the seventh floor. She stepped out. 777 was at the very end of the hall. She gingerly made her way toward the room with her hand on her gun, turning to look behind her. The adrenalin was pumping. Her eyes were saucers, and her senses were that of a cat in a yard of dogs. Eventually, she arrived at the door and scanned the key. It was now or never. She burst through the door with her pistol drawn only to find a lavish dinner table adorned with formalwear, champagne, and accoutréments. At the end of the table was Bradley Finny, dressed in a handsome white suit. She stood there pointing the gun at him, but he didn't move. He just sat staring blankly ahead without even addressing or acknowledging her.

"Mr. Finny? Hello?"

He continued staring blankly ahead and not looking at her. Bradley approached cautiously, and as she got close to him, she could see something was wrong. She moved around behind him and could see blood coming through his white suit. She pushed him forward and stepped back. He slumped onto the table, and she leapt forward to check his pulse. He was dead, and he'd been stabbed through the back just inside his left shoulder blade, the same as Scattergood and the LA guy. *What the hell was this?* Bradley's thoughts were swimming. She was at sea. She was about to get out of the room when she noticed an envelope on the floor that had dropped down when Finny slumped forward. She picked it up and opened it. It was a handwritten note.

My name is Bradley Finny. I am in fear for my life. I am being pursued by a lady called Madeline Bradley, and I think she is trying to kill me.

"What the fuck is going on here? I've gotta get the fuck out."

Bradley slid the note into her pocket and ran to the door. Hanging the do-not-disturb sign on the door handle to buy herself some time, she swiftly made her way back to her room, packed her bag, and headed to the lobby. The hotel manager saw her and smiled.

"Everything alright, mademoiselle?"

"Yes, it is fine; I've just been called away. All is well. I have to fly home urgently."

"Très bien. Bonne soirée, mademoiselle."

Nine Fine Deaths

Bradley got in a taxi that was waiting in the street outside the hotel and asked him to drive to Nice Airport as fast as possible.

Having a few moments to think, she started going through possibilities. *What could possibly be happening? Who could be behind this? If Bradley Finny was not the killer, who was behind this whole thing?* She was back to square one, and she was out of her mind with worry and wonder. She had to get back to Merrick and work out what to do. If European authorities got hold of her, she was screwed. Even worse, Monaco authorities. She could not even imagine the hell she'd be in.

"Detective Bradley," came a refined but disturbing voice from the driver's seat.

"Have we met?" said Bradley, masking her terror while slowly getting her hand on her gun.

"Well, not officially, no, but we have worked together for some time."

"The person responsible for my hasty exit from Monaco, do I take it?"

"Yes, but fear not, the evidence that links you is superficial and circumstantial. I just thought it would heighten the adventure. Your dinner date-to-be bookended our decade-long dalliance. I do like a tidy affair. I really must thank you for such a grand participation. I do feel like we have worked so beautifully together."

"What the fuck are you talking about. You realize you sound completely delusional?"

"Oh, come now, my dear Detective. It's not like we have not worked closely. We've even been face-to-face a few times. Do you not recognize the illustrious Miss Fanny bird in my vocal timber," changing his voice into his elderly financier persona. "I am sorry I had to bankrupt you and cause your indictment, but it was the only way to lead you to your true calling, Detective Bradley of Homicide."

Bradley slid over slightly, trying to get a better look at the mysterious figure driving the car, but his face was obscured by a hood.

"You best not get a look at my face, m' dear; that would not bode well for you. Now that our affairs are complete, I have no need to call on your services in the future, and you'll have no need to pursue me."

"How about I just shoot you right now?"

"That would not bode well for your parents in Brixham, would it? I assure you that measures are in place to irradicate them should I not be available to cease activities. I just wanted us to have a nice chat before parting ways. You see, murder is art, but art is so much richer and more deeply enjoyed if shared. You have been my art appreciation companion. My motivation, as it were."

"I see, you're insane. But why Bradley Finny? It makes no sense to have killed him."

"No loose ends, you see. First off, his name is not Bradley Finny. My name is Bradley Finny. Well, one of my aliases, at least. My real name, for intents and purposes, is Bradbury Leigh Fine. Some call me Brad Leigh. A pleasure to make your acquaintance.

Eleven years ago, while staying at a hotel in Puerta Vallarta under one of my pseudonyms, Bradley Finny. A young gentleman decided to use my name and room number to oblige himself of my hospitality in the restaurant and bar of the hotel. I discovered it right away as the hotel manager, who knew me, asked what was going on, but I asked him not to interfere and told him that I knew the gentleman and I was conducting an experiment. The truth is, I wanted to surveil him and see if he had any real skill or was just a two-bit punk scamming a meal. I was losing interest quickly when suddenly he approached you, Miss Bradley. A chance meeting that turned into an overnight dalliance. Funded by me, incidentally, you're most welcome. He was slick but quite the bore, but you, you intrigued me. You opened up like a blossoming flower and shared your innermost thoughts, demons, and dreams—which, I surmised, was quite out of character for you—and with some carefully selected seating choices plus a device or two, it all happened within earshot of me. Your mind so inspired me. I knew you would make a fine accomplice, but I had a lot to do if I were going to make it work.

Obviously, in the morning, he made a hasty escape so as not to be apprehended for charging up a princely sum to my room account. I tracked him down living in London, and I warded him off pursuing you, pretending to be a jealous husband. A decade later, I saw the opportunity to use him again, so I made contact with him, and by pretending to be you, I had him hopping. You left quite the impression on him.

It was me who left the chocolates on your pillow in London and arranged for him to come looking for you. I then sent him a message from you asking you to meet him in Monaco for dinner in your suite. He arrived at the suite at 6:45 giving me time to wrap things up before your arrival.

So, there you have it. That was the life and times of Mr. Harold Price. Petty conman and thief. Handsome, though, I'll give him that. It's a pity you never got to enjoy him in full."

"And Dr. Johannah Mayor. What did she do to attract your not-so-kind attention?"

"Ah, Dr. Mayor. She was to be my first, you see. My debut as an artist. Unfortunately, I was interrupted and lost my nerve some decades earlier. Some years after that, I had another misfire with Miss Whitney Ricks, AKA Alexis Anna

Riccardi. I first met Miss Ricks in Hollywood in '79, but a voyeuristic onlooker named Reynaldo Sanchez disturbed us, unfortunately for him. Imagine my surprise when walking into a diamond merchant on 47th St over twenty years later to find the ever-enchanting Miss Ricks-Riccardi working in the fine diamond business. That single instant reignited my passion and desire to fulfill my dream as an artist of death. And Dr. Mayor, well, she'd seen my face. She only knew me as Darby Finn, but I couldn't have her stumbling across me somewhere and being able to identify me."

"And Miss Scattergood?"

"Ah, Miss Scattergood, well, I needed a reason to get you to London for my full plan to be realized, and I remembered she was a vexation of yours, so I thought I'd do you a little favor while delivering my tour de art on her naked flesh. It could have been anyone, but that bitch just had to die."

"Well, no argument there. But why all women? Do you have something against women?"

"Quite the opposite. Women are art. Murdering men just lacks style. Mr. Sanchez was an unfortunate hurdle. He had seen me. He had to be disposed of. I just stuck him with my ice pick and left him be. No art there. It was East LA, after all."

"But what about Alexei Freeman? Where's your man rule there?"

"I didn't kill Mr. Freeman. His student, Miss Nistratov, did so under the instruction of her father, Alexander Nistratov, who had lost his lucrative art counterfeiting operation thanks to Mr. Freeman's discovery. Talia Nistratov turned up to poison Freeman, and I turned up to kill and pose Miss Nistratov in that lurid sexual sculpture to enrage her father. I just can't allow people to corrupt the art world with their disgraceful forgeries just so they can launder money. It's just rude, you know. Unacceptable."

"Yes, I see you're most diligent about doing the right thing. So, Dearborn, Wheeler, and Roosevelt?"

"Just people I meet while going about my business. You know, when the mood strikes. It's not just about the attractiveness of the subject for my art; it's the art of execution, the how. It's about gaining access. Being invited in. My love for art takes me all over the world and into the homes of all sorts of people. Roosevelt was extraordinary. I knew her separately from you and thought she would make a wonderful exhibit. The fact that she had wronged you was a little cherry on the top. Anyhow, here we are at the airport. You'll be off to Madrid, I'll be off to my destination, and a lovely fellow, currently in the trunk, can resume his duties as cab driver.

Again, a perfect closed loop. Very tidy. It has been a pleasure. I do hope you'll look back on our adventures with a fond smile from time to time. Be well now; best not we keep company."

Bradley was speechless as she stepped out of the cab.

"By the way, the ride is on me," quipped the cloaked mystery man as he pulled the cab out from the curb and went on his way.

Bradley walked her bag slowly into the terminal in surreal bewilderment. Sure enough, there was a flight to Madrid—in half an hour—from where she could fly direct to New York. She bought a ticket for the flight and ran to the gate, where she waited anxiously to board before the body was discovered back in Monaco.

All the way home, she was thinking about what she was going to say to Captain Merrick. What a mess she was in. Then it occurred to her. She could blame the whole thing on Bradley Finny, whom she killed with an ice pick in self-defense after discovering he was the serial killer. *She fled the scene, knowing she would be detained indefinitely so that she could get back to the safety and authority of her home base.* It was perfect. She knew if she pursued the actual killer, her life and the lives of her parents, and really anyone she knew, would be in danger. This was the only way. She landed at JFK, and as she walked off the jetway, she was met by Captain Merrick and two uniformed officers who took her into custody.

"Bradley, I don't know what the hell went down over there, but there is a dead body and an ice pick with your fingerprints all over it."

"There is? Yes, there is, Captain," immediately realizing that this is what this maniac had planned; he *put my fingerprints on the murder weapon somehow.* "I got him, Captain. His name is Bradley Finny, and he is the serial killer."

"And I suppose you can back all this up, Bradley?"

"What's to back up? He invited me to Monaco and was planning to kill me. I got in first."

"Bradley, only you could make my life this complicated. Ok, guys, let her go, we will work this out back at the station."

Over the following weeks, Bradley worked hard to connect this nobody to all of the murders while concealing the truth. Fortunately, Harold Price—the imposter Bradley Finny she's met—being a criminal meant it was very hard to dig up any evidence on him that countered the web of lies Bradley was spinning. She did such a good job of connecting nonexistent dots that Captain Merrick commended her detective work. She discovered things about Harold Price that could have put him anywhere in the world at any time. From being able to enter and exit countries undetected to having developed refined skills at entering and exiting buildings as a burglar. Pinning nine murders on him was so easy; it was like she was being helped.

Bradley thought long and hard about what to do next. Could she live in a world knowing that there was somebody out there who had done these despicable things? Was she even safe from future plans that he might suddenly dream up? Over the coming year, her daily focus on everything that had happened began to diminish until she would only think about it from time to time. Her career went from strength to strength, and she was now highly decorated and regarded as one of the best in the city. The country, even. She even started to behave herself a little and treat, at least some, people with a modicum of respect.

Two years had passed, and life was good for Bradley. One day, while working a case on the Upper East Side, she decided to stroll through her old neighborhood. Fifth Avenue, Madison, Park, The Mark Hotel on East 77th St. A thoroughly enjoyable sunny New York afternoon stroll. She didn't even notice it at first. She'd walked past it hundreds of times and sometimes even admired pieces in the window. Her brain must have caught it from the corner of her eye. Right there on 77th St was an art store, and the name was not a description, as she had always thought, it was a name. Fine Art. She stood there looking through the window motionless. Thoughts shot through her head. Should she just keep walking? *Hey, this is just an art store on the Upper East Side. What's the harm in wandering in? I am, after all, an art admirer. Or so I've been told.*

Bradley walked into the store. The door had one of those quaint little bells that alerted the store owner to visitors. Standing towards the back of the store, facing the other way, was a very well-dressed woman. Bradley walked up slowly and stopped just behind her. The woman was admiring a painting on the back wall but turned around when she realized there was a figure to her right.

"Oh, I'm sorry, I was lost in thought," said the articulate, refined woman.

"Oh, not at all. Are you the owner?"

"No, I am just a humble curator in the employ of the owner."

"Is the owner here?"

"Good heavens, no. We never see Mr. Fine. He just sends his instructions, and we do his bidding. Do you know, I've never even seen him?"

"Intriguing. Well, I was just wondering. I've walked by so many times and never realized that Fine Art was more than a description. It was morbid curiosity that led me to want to meet the Mr. Fine in Fine Art. Never mind. I'll be on my way."

The curator stood watching Bradley leave, thinking to herself, *that was odd. Never mind.*

Bradley walked back to her car and drove toward home, deciding to investigate no further but content that she had at least uncovered another important clue. Hopefully, Mr. Fine would be none the wiser. As far as she was concerned, their understanding was intact.

The End

But there are more fine
adventures to follow

www.ingramcontent.com/pod-product-compliance
Lightning Source LLC
Chambersburg PA
CBHW030335020726
47493CB00004B/1283